. . . . .

MY MOTHER PULLS A CIGARETTE FROM THE SUN VISOR AND lights it in her mouth, so I roll my window down and stick my head out. I can see all the stars I rarely ever looked at until we came to Montauk Point. *I see you now, stars. Do you see me? I was a nobody. But I've been working so hard, so hard, to be one of you.*

Unscripted
Joss Byrd

Unscripted Joss Byrd

a novel

LYGIA DAY PEÑAFLOR

SQUARE
FISH
ROARING BROOK PRESS
New York

SQUARE FISH

An imprint of Macmillan
175 Fifth Avenue
New York, NY 10010
fiercereads.com

Square Fish and the Square Fish logo are trademarks of Macmillan and
are used by Roaring Brook Press under license from Macmillan.

Our books may be purchased in bulk for promotional, educational, or business use. Please
contact your local bookseller or the Macmillan Corporate and Premium Sales Department
at (800) 221-7945 ext. 5442 or by e-mail at MacmillanSpecialMarkets@macmillan.com.

Library of Congress Cataloging-in-Publication Data

Names: Peñaflor, Lygia Day, author.
Title: Unscripted Joss Byrd / Lygia Day Peñaflor.
Description: New York : Roaring Brook Press, 2016. | Summary: Joss Byrd, Americas
    most sought-after young actress, navigates the personal pressures of working on a
    new film and staying true to herself.
Identifiers: LCCN 2015039824 | ISBN 978-1-250-11516-4 (paperback) |
    ISBN 978-1-62672-370-2 (ebook)
Subjects: | CYAC: Actors and actresses—Fiction. | Self-actualization—Fiction. |
    BISAC: JUVENILE FICTION / Performing Arts / Film. | JUVENILE FICTION /
    Social Issues / Self-Esteem & Self-Reliance.
Classification: LCC PZ7.1.P4454 Un 2016 | DDC [Fic]—dc23
LC record available at https://lccn.loc.gov/2015039824

Originally published in the United States by Roaring Brook Press
First Square Fish edition, 2017
Square Fish logo designed by Filomena Tuosto

1   3   5   7   9   10   8   6   4   2

AR: 4.2 / LEXILE: HL620L

*For all the showbiz kids who've spent three hours
a day with me without complaining (much)*

1

VIVA, MY MOTHER, IS KNEADING JERGENS LOTION INTO HER skin until it soaks through her pores. The cream turns from white to clear as she works it into her heels. She pumps the bottle with a squish and rubs her elbows and hands, her neck, and the parts of her back she can reach under her T-shirt. "Beauty depends upon a strict routine," she sighs, patting a potion from a dark purple jar under her eyes. "Men will never know all we go through." Then she swipes Vaseline over her lips before reaching for her bedtime cigarette.

"Okay." She drops the script beside me on her way out the door. "We'll do it again when I get back."

Every night we run the dialogue for the next day. My mother does the boys' parts in quick bursts, the way Chris and Jericho would say them, while I try to squeeze the right words from my brain. Tonight it's scene 15: me and the boys build a crow's nest.

In the next room, there are little kids—it sounds like three brothers—wrestling. Each time they thud against our wall they yell, "Off the ropes!" I've always wanted a big brother—the kind who would pull our dog in a red wagon and stick up for me against bullies on the playground. I get to have a big brother in this script. Chris Tate plays TJ, and I play Norah. TJ sticks up for Norah against our stepdad, but we don't get a dog or a wagon.

Other than the thin walls, the Beachcomber Resort is pretty nice. The doors open up to the outside landing. My mother likes to watch TV sets flicker in the rooms across the pool while she smokes. She says she likes to guess at what people are watching. I might have a good ten minutes to close my eyes.

The door clicks, waking me from a shallow sleep. My mother shakes her smoky hair into the room. "Ready?"

I lift my head and turn a page in my yellow script to make her think I've been practicing. On the nightstand, pink and blue scripts with ripped and curled corners lie under Viva's coffee cups. It's hard for me to learn script changes. Thankfully we've been filming the yellow version for weeks, so I'm finally all right with it. For the most part.

"You'd better get all the way through this time. No stopping," Viva says.

I flip the bedsheets over my legs.

"Seriously, Joss." She nudges me with her knee and picks up the script. "Let's do this before you fall asleep. You haven't even brushed your teeth yet."

I force my tired self to sit up. Filming three scenes today

wasn't exactly a day at the beach, even though we are at the beach. I couldn't wait to get here to shoot outdoors. Filming for two months inside a dark studio in Brooklyn gave me cabin fever, as Viva said. But we've been in Montauk for a week now, and I haven't played in the water once. I've barely dipped my toes in it. And I haven't been to Montauk Lighthouse even though Terrance, my director, promised to take me there. If I buy a postcard of Montauk Point for a keepsake, it'll be a lie because all the postcards are pictures of the lighthouse.

"Okay." Viva holds the script and clears her throat. "All we'll have to do is climb up here every morning, and we'll be able to see right away how the waves are," she reads Chris's line. "No more trekking our boards all the way down to the beach at six in the morning when the water's flat."

"We'll never have to walk down to the shore again," I say my line and yawn. "Can we please finish this in the morning?" I ask my mother. "I'm so done right now."

"You have five days left on this shoot, and *then* you'll be done."

I lie down and curl into a little ball.

"Sit up." Viva catches my ankle, but I kick away and grab at the sheets to cover myself.

"I don't want to do it anymore." I clutch my head. I'll focus better in the morning.

She slams the script on the desk. "You don't wanna *do* it anymore?"

3

I shouldn't push my luck, but my crankiness is taking over. "No!"

"No?" She pulls my blankets off, leaving me cold. "Why are we here, then, huh? If you don't wanna *do* it anymore?" She swings around the room, pulls my suitcase off the dresser, and throws it onto the bed.

"What are you doing?" I sit up against the headboard.

She's grabbing pajamas off the bed, snatching sneakers up from the floor and dirty clothes off a chair.

"Pack your things!" Viva yells as she throws everything into the bag. "You don't wanna do it anymore? So don't."

I shield myself with the pillow. "That's not what I meant!"

"You think I do this for *me*? You think I enjoy sitting around all day long watching everybody treat you like you're Shirley Temple? You don't think I have better things to do with *my* life?" She runs to the kitchenette and pulls the cereal boxes, chips, and canned soup off the counter. "I could be developing my business idea right now and selling it to stores all over the country. Nobody else is making dancewear that doubles as shapewear." She shoves the groceries into the suitcase on top of underwear and magazines. "But no. I'm here securing a future for you, and you don't wanna *do* it anymore?"

I groan into my pillow. "I just want to go to sleep!"

"Well, good. Now you can sleep all you want. At *home*." She slaps the suitcase shut. "And you can go to sixth grade and sit in the Reading Resource Room for the whole year if that's what you want."

I stare at her, shocked. That's the meanest thing she can say to me without flat-out calling me dumb. I wait for her to apologize and take it back. But her hard eyes are miles and miles away from being sorry. The thought of the Reading Resource Room makes me sick—those faded cartoon wall signs of kids reading under blankets, at picnics, at the beach—BOOKS ARE FUN!

Viva straightens her shoulders and shoves the suitcase toward me. "Pack!" She grabs her purse and keys off the dresser and storms out of Beachcomber room 204 and down the wooden stairs.

When my mother acts crazy, I do as she says. Crazy beats cranky any night. I kneel on the bed and stuff my bags with Cap'n Crunch and string cheese, jeans and sweatpants. Two loud honks snap me to my feet. The suitcase, with shirtsleeves and a cheddar popcorn bag sticking out, can only zip so far, so I lug the sloppy bag out the door and down the steps in my bare feet, leaving the script behind.

I cross in front of our truck. The heat from its headlights feels like movie lights. I stop and soak up the warmth for a second, and the lines I'd been memorizing tumble from my lips. "All's we need now is a pair of binoculars. Then we can see clear through to the lighthouse. Don't you think?" I whisper and wait for Viva to turn the engine off.

"Let's go!" my mother yells. The horn shakes my whole body and vibrates in my chest.

I hurl my suitcase into the truck, and then I push empty water bottles and burger wrappers aside in the passenger seat.

With pebbles and sand stuck to the soles of my feet, we pull out in silence toward the road, where two guys from our movie crew are walking up from the beach.

"Well, if it isn't Viva and Joss Byrd. Where are you two going at this hour?" one of them asks, but my mother only looks forward and drives ahead.

Six . . . seven . . . eight . . . nine . . . I measure our distance from the resort by counting the streetlamps. Viva is playing chicken, and I don't know how to win. Am I supposed to jump out? Or pretend not to care and let her drive into the night until she decides enough is enough? I'll be sleepwalking on set tomorrow. She'll blame me even though it'll be her fault.

Thirteen . . . fourteen . . . fifteen . . . sixteen . . . We pass stables and motels, a gas station, a diner, froufrou-la-di-da Long Island houses with glass walls that face the ocean, and driveways behind vine-covered gates. Maybe she means it, and we're really going home. Maybe she wants to remind me of what it's like to be a nobody just to teach me a lesson. If I don't show up to work in the morning no one will ever hire me again.

Viva wouldn't dare. She wouldn't dare.

Twenty-two . . . twenty-three . . . When I was six, my mother decided to chase a hunch and took us on a car trip. In every way, that drive was the exact opposite of this one.

Thirty . . . thirty-one . . .

. . . . .

"I can feel it, Joss. It's a sign. A sign. Untitled Feature Film: Open Call for Girls, Ages 5–7." My mother tears the ad from the newspaper and slaps it on the kitchen table.

"What are the odds I'd see this today? I mean, when do I ever actually read the newspaper, right?" She crouches as if she's about to tell me a secret. "I only buy it for the coupons."

She circles the bottom of the ad while dialing the phone. "Hey, Viva here. Sorry, but I'm not coming in today. Yeah . . . my kid's sick." She winks at me. We're in cahoots. But I'm not sure what for. "I don't know. Something with a lot of mucus."

I make a face.

Viva sticks out her tongue. "I should probably take her to the doctor."

The ad has a drawing of a movie camera in the middle. I look it over as my mother pretends to write down the number for a doctor.

"Take the books out of your backpack and put some snacks in," she says, hanging up the phone.

"Why?" I ask, already smiling. "I'm not going to school?"

"No. We're driving to New York. You're gonna audition for this movie. And you're gonna get it, too. Don't you feel it?" my mother says, searching the kitchen for her keys.

For some reason I picture myself singing and dancing with a cane. "Okay!" Skipping school is all right by me. I empty my bag down to the last dirty penny and shove my whole box of Lucky Charms inside it.

"You didn't drink anything yet, did you?" She shuffles me out the door. *"'Cause we're not stopping till we get there, baby!"*

At the Lobster Roll, my mother pulls into the parking lot; late-night diners are stepping out of the restaurant patting their bellies. There must be chowder and oyster crackers in there. I imagine Terrance Rivenbach and Peter Bustamante, my direc-tor and executive producer, sitting inside with bibs on. I want to run in and tell them that Viva's kidnapping me, that it isn't my idea to go. I imagine them sending my mother away but letting me stay. The waiter would give me a bib, and Terrance and Peter and me would clink lobster claws together as Viva drove away. I'd stay in the hotel room by myself and go to the set alone and shoot my scenes without her watching me. I could breathe without her telling me the right way to do it.

My mother pulls a cigarette from the sun visor and lights it in her mouth, so I roll my window down and stick my head out. I can see all the stars I rarely ever looked at until we came to Montauk Point. *I see you now, stars. Do you see me? I was a no-body. But I've been working so hard, so hard, to be one of you.*

. . . . .

"We're gonna find you the best agent in Hollywood." My mother is talking too loudly for the library. She wants people to hear that I got the part of Tallulah Leigh, and I'm gonna be in a movie. *"An agent for real actors, the serious ones—you know, like the*

Fannings—kids who work with Sandra Bullock and Matt Damon. Not Disney actors." She taps the keys on the computer and scrolls through pictures of kids with tiny words beside them. "We have to find someone big. Big! A real mover and shaker. And then we'll be on our—Bingo!"

She smiles her jackpot smile and starts dialing her cell. It's embarrassing when she turns on the speakerphone. The old man who's reading a newspaper and the lady behind the horseshoe desk are staring at us.

"Creative Team Management."

"May I speak with Doris Cole please?" My mother grabs my arm. "This is Viva Byrd, mother of Joss Byrd." Wink. "She's playing Tallulah Leigh in the film Hit the Road.*"*

"Please hold."

My mother whispers, "She's going to make you a star!"

"Ms. Byrd! This is Doris Cole. I've been expecting your call," Doris says, because that's the kind of mover and shaker she is.

· · · · ·

"So?" Viva says now, staring into the window of the Lobster Roll. "Where are we going?"

When I pull my head back inside and stare at my bare feet that don't quite touch the mat, I feel poor—poor and sad and small. "Back to the hotel," I answer, because I don't want to be a nobody again, and if we go back to our apartment in Tyrone, Pennsylvania, I will be.

9

"And this is what *you* want?" she asks, exhaling heavy smoke out the window.

I want to feel full and rich inside, the way I feel when the French toast on set is soft and warm, made especially for me, and when a wardrobe girl gives me ankle boots and designer jeans with the tags still on, even when I know they aren't for keeps.

I look back at the road. "Yes."

Viva dangles her cigarette over the steering wheel. "Will I ever have to force you to do the work again?"

I shake my head.

She turns to face me; there are creases around her mouth I never noticed before. "I can't hear you."

"No."

She pelts her cigarette like a dart out the window. Dust whirls into the air when she turns the truck around.

Twenty-seven . . . twenty-six . . . twenty-five . . . On the way back to the Beachcomber, I count the lampposts backward and hope that when I get down to zero, this night will subtract into nothing, too.

I remember that first time we spoke with Doris Cole over the speakerphone. She told us that her clients are the "cream of the crop." She said, "No pageant princesses, no jazz hands, just real kids with honest-to-goodness talent." By the end of that first phone call, Viva and Doris and me were all on a first-name basis. "Partners." That's what my mother called us.

And I was rising to the top. I just hope that someone lets me know the second I get there because it's gotta be better than this.

. . . . .

Wouldn't you know that now that I'm in my pajamas, I'm not sleepy anymore. I've already brushed my teeth and washed my face, so now I'm just running the water to sound busy. It's all I can do to get some privacy. The bathroom is the only alone time I get around here. I poke around Viva's makeup bag and use a little bit of her lip balm from a tiny red tin. If there's an expiration date for makeup, it's definitely passed. The blush and eye shadow don't have covers, and her lipsticks have mismatched caps. I don't know why she shaves the pencils into the bag instead of into the trash.

Finally I open the door. Viva pats the space beside her on her bed. "Come." I guess we're cool again; we're back to normal. But I wait for a second. I'm not that easy to win back. "Aw, come on, crawl in," she says.

Even though my mother has brushed her teeth, her whole being still smells like cigarettes. I settle in next to her and think about how she might seem so much younger if she didn't smoke or if she ran errands in workout clothes and a ponytail like some of the other mothers, instead of jeans and high heels and lots of makeup. Sometimes I leave magazine pages around the house with pictures of "On-the-Go Celebrity Moms" who look fit in yoga pants and shop at a store called Whole Foods, but Viva doesn't get the hint.

"Whaddaya say we take our spending money and have ourselves some of that lobster tomorrow night?" she asks in a gravelly voice.

Nodding into her chest, I curl against her shape.

"Didn't that place look yum? We could get dressed up, you could get a Shirley Temple, I could get a nice wine. We can people watch. You'd like that, wouldn't you?"

The name Shirley Temple makes me cringe. I don't think my mother even remembers half the things she says when she's angry.

"Oh, I know what else we could do," she says soothingly as she reaches for her laptop. Inside her T-shirt, her heavy, loose boobs fall toward the mattress.

When my first movie came out, critics called me the "next Tatum O'Neal." Since I didn't know who that was, Doris told us to study Tatum O'Neal in a movie called *Paper Moon*. That's what Doris said—not "watch" but "study." That made it sound real important. Right away, I didn't think I'd like the movie because it was in black and white. But when I took a good look at Tatum mouthing off line after line after line without missing a beat, I could've sworn that she was in color. I've studied *Paper Moon* so many times that I know all of Tatum's lines. She's the best actor in the movie, even better than her own dad, who's in it, too.

To be honest, I would've been happy to be called just an okay actor instead of the next Tatum O'Neal. Critics really put the pressure on.

"Fully charged. We're in luck." My mother wakes the DVD. It starts right back up from where we left off. We bought our laptop when I got my first job. It's definitely time for a new one.

"You see that spark in Tatum's eye? That's what won her an Oscar." My mother's comments weave in and out at the usual places. I've memorized her lines just as good as Tatum's. "There's the scene . . . right there. The gold standard. Such a big attitude in that little body."

I press my head deep into my pillow. Tatum's close-up is all tears and freckles.

"She's so scrappy. That's what everybody sees in you."

That's why you have to work as much as you can . . .

"That's why you have to work as much as you can while it's still cute to be scrappy. We have to ride this wave as long as possible."

Just ride it and ride it and ride it . . .

"Just ride it and ride it and ride it."

Doris says that puberty can be the end of a child actor. Girls who stay petite and flat can play young parts for a very long time. But if you've seen my mother, who's tall and definitely not flat, you know that probably won't happen for me.

The laptop settles on my mother's stomach as she stretches her legs. "Tatum was lucky. It was easy for her to transition to

13

teen roles because she grew up beautiful. But you might, you might not. If we save every penny now you won't have to worry about it either way."

I'll worry no matter what. Savings or no savings, if I have to grow up at all, I'd like to grow up beautiful.

"And if you work enough now, you definitely won't have to struggle when you're my age. Look at those eyes . . . God, that Tatum . . ."

After I'd studied the movie too many times to count, Doris told me that *Paper Moon* could've been shot in color, but it was made in black and white on purpose, to be more believable. Who knew? That's another thing I learned from *Paper Moon* besides how to be scrappy: you can get away with anything if you do it on purpose. The way I figure it, as long as I keep a straight face, people will believe that I'm a real actor, when really all I am is a kid who wanted to skip school that first day.

"Nobody ever pushed me. Nobody ever thought I was worth pushing. You have something, Joss. You really do," Viva says, adding new words to her comments. "And the fact that you have these opportunities . . . well, who would've imagined?" She's braiding my hair like she used to when I was little. "I just don't want you to waste all of this. I wish you could understand that." She lets the braid loose and combs through it with her fingers. "Life's hard enough when you haven't got a talent. I should know. I don't want your life to be hard."

When I take a long, deep breath, I can make out the sweet

14

smell of my mother's lotion hiding beneath her stale layer of smoke. Tatum singing is the last thing I hear before I fall asleep. Her voice almost convinces me that everything will be just grand.

"Keep your sunny side up, up. Hide the side that gets blue!"

2

"I'm so happy to meet you, Joss. I've watched Hit the Road *a dozen times. You're so good in it. So good."* Terrance Rivenbach, the famous director, hugs me with both arms. *"Can I tell you a secret?"* He has twinkly eyes; that's my favorite kind of face. All at once I'm nervous. I don't know how to talk to someone who's more handsome in person than he is on the Internet. *"You're the only Norah I want."* He winks.

Terrance's office is full of boxes. All that's out are file folders, pictures of his family, and a coffeemaker. *"Let's sit down, Joss. Sorry. This is a new building. We're all just getting settled."* We walk around the boxes to get to the chairs near the window. *"How do you like LA?"* He smiles kindly and hands me a warm bottle of water from a box.

I uncap the bottle but don't drink. *"Fine."*

"It's a long way from Tyrone, Pennsylvania. Think you'll want to come live here someday?" He tilts his head toward the window. *"You're getting awfully busy filming movies."*

"I guess." I peel the label off my water. I should tell him that it's

our goal—Viva's and mine—to live in Beverly Hills. Our favorite houses are the ones with ivy up the sides. You can tell they've stood there since what Viva calls the Golden Age of Hollywood, which was when "darn" was a curse, people kept their clothes on, and the camera faded after kissing. Even if you just moved into your ivy house, you can pretend that you've had money since the Golden Age. But I don't say any of that to Terrance.

"How do you like acting?"

It's the one thing, the only thing that makes me special, *I think. "It's good," I say. I'm failing the interview already.* Damn.

· · · · ·

Every day in Montauk the cast-and-crew van shuttles us between the Beachcomber and our production basecamp and our filming location. This morning I have rehearsal first. Then I'll tutor for a while before we shoot. Our driver is following the handmade TO SET signs that lead us through narrower and narrower streets of tiny beach houses. When we pull up to what's supposed to be TJ and Norah's house, the crew is hauling equipment to the backyard. I'm embarrassed straight off by this rickety place with a dirt driveway because everyone's been saying that I'm perfect for the part of Norah. How can they tell I really am a dirt-driveway kid? (That is, if I had a driveway.) And I'm also embarrassed for Terrance because the character TJ is based on him as a kid; *The Locals* is about him, his actual sister, Norah, his actual evil stepdad, and his actual dumpy house. Why would somebody who's rich want the world to know that he used to be poor?

17

"Uh-oh! Here comes trouble!" In the backyard, a happy Terrance holds his arms open. "Look out, Montauk!" He squeezes me so tight—the exact way he hugged me when we first met—that I can smell his aftershave and his morning coffee.

I squeeze him right back. "Morning, Terrance."

"When are you going to start calling me TJ?" he asks. But I can't call him that. TJ is a kid's name—a boy with a rainbow lollipop.

If you've ever met Terrance Rivenbach you'd never guess he grew up in a shack. I can tell you one thing: the minute Viva and me dig our way out of the hole we're in, we aren't gonna look back. We're in what my mother calls a "steaming pile of debt without a shovel." It's stupid that we're in debt because we haven't got anything good. I mean it—nothing. For such a long time, I've wanted this pair of chunky headphones that I can use on plane rides. But all Viva can say is, "What do you need those for? They're ridiculous." I want them because they would cancel out noise—her voice, for example—when I need my privacy.

Thanks to Viva's ex-boyfriend, all we do have are empty plots of land because his master plan to build upscale beauty salons was a bust. We also have a hole in our bank account where there used to be my movie money. When my mother's not screwing it up, I don't mind earning money for us. I really don't. I like being useful. It's called being the breadwinner. But that's what made losing my movie money feel ten times worse.

"Take a look at these." Terrance hands me a sheet of pictures from my photo shoot the other day. Me and Chris were made up to look like an old photo of Terrance and his sister when they were little. "Here's the original. And here's you two," he says, holding both photos.

"We look exactly like you!"

In the original, Terrance and Norah are in the middle of the street. He's straddling his bicycle, and Norah, wearing rainbow shorts, is pinching her elbow and staring straight into the camera with a bubble wand between her teeth. In our new photo, me and Chris are positioned just the same.

"Amazing, isn't it?" Terrance points from his picture to mine. "This is going to be our poster."

I look over at Chris. He's by the snack table reading today's call sheet, which tells the scenes we're filming and in what order. "Hey, Chris! Cool, huh?"

"I know, right?" There's dirt on his palm when he lifts his hand. Judging from the scrapes on Chris's elbows and the smudges on his face, it looks like he's been rehearsing already.

Rodney, the actor who plays our evil stepdad, keeps staring at me from inside the screen door. I smile at him, only because I'm used to being polite. But there's no charming Rodney.

"You know he likes to stay in character." Terrance slips the photos into a big Ziploc bag. "Just let him be."

Rodney likes to stay in character so much that his name isn't even Rodney. It's Tom Garrett. But we aren't supposed to use that name at all; it even says "Rodney" on call sheets and memos where the rest of us have our real names.

He might only be acting, but Rodney's still plenty scary. When my mother told me *The Locals* was about a girl who gets abused by her stepdad, I said, "No way. No how." I didn't want some strange man acting dirty with me. Good thing Viva felt the same. She said everybody draws the line somewhere. Plus, she figured a kid like me with a few movies in my pocket should have a say-so in my own career. So she and Doris fixed my contract so I wouldn't have to do any pervy scenes. That was a major relief, especially the second I got a look at Rodney. According to Google, he used to be a pro football player. That explains his giant hands and his beer gut. I think that when athletes stop playing their muscles melt into their bellies.

Anyway, Viva said that the contract would protect me from "content of a sexual or violent nature as deemed by the minor's parent and management." She also told me that for once, I'd get to work with other kids on this movie. That sealed the deal for me, even if there is a pervy stepdad.

Terrance walks me over to a tall, fat tree that shades half the backyard. "Joss, for this scene, I want you to sit up here in this big old tree."

"Yes!" I pat the tree like an old friend, excited to spend the day in it. It's a heavy-duty scene, but more so for Chris. For me, it'll be fun being up in the tree.

"You'll watch TJ and Buzz drill the rungs into the trunk from up here," he says. "And we'll do some nice close-ups on you right before Chris gets roughed up."

Chris is roughed up already. The medic is cleaning him up with alcohol pads.

"We'll put some padding up here to make it comfortable," Terrance says as I pull myself up by the low branches.

"Whoa, not yet." He grabs hold of my arm. "Let's save the climb for later. You're not allowed to break your neck until after we wrap."

"But it's easy." I look up through the flat leaves rustling above. "It's not even that high."

"It's high enough."

"Joss, you're so lucky you get to be up in the tree!" says Jericho. He plays Buzz, TJ's best friend. I thought the hair department was going to give Jericho a buzz cut, but I guess that's not where the name comes from; he's still shaggy as ever. "Look what I get! A saw!" Jericho lifts a rusty saw from against the tree and holds it for me to see.

"Hey, hey! Put it down!" Terrance yells, getting serious. "You have to get instructions on that first. There was a reason for the safety memo this morning. No props until I say so. If there's any fooling around on this set, I'll shut it down. That goes for all of you. Clear?"

"Aye, aye, Cap'n." Jericho lowers the saw back to the ground.

I don't get Jericho. *The Locals* is only his first movie, but he fools around all the time as if he's been acting forever. I'm never that comfortable on set. My theory is he's relaxed because he's a hobby actor. That's what I call a kid who's the opposite of a breadwinner—a kid who works for fun, not for money, which must be way less stressful. While I bring home the bacon, hobby actors bring home stories about famous people to tell around the dinner table. I can tell a hobby actor from a mile away. I've noticed Jericho's dad working with color-coded graphs on his laptop and heard him make business calls on "Tokyo Time." He also wears a watch that can go underwater. Jericho said so.

"For now, just play with the dialogue for a bit before I see it," Terrance says.

Viva is standing off to the side with the executive producer, Peter Bustamante. After three movies, I still don't know what a producer does. It's too late to ask, so I just pretend to know. But I'm plenty interested in any job where you walk around acting like the boss but never actually do anything. Peter doesn't work any equipment or even carry a script.

Viva gives me a wave. She likes to remind big-deal people that she's my mother. I wave back. I like to remind big-deal people that I'm a good daughter; Doris says that being pleasing on set is as important as being talented.

Tonight will be a fancy dinner night, for sure; Viva looks in a good mood. But before I can say *Lobster Roll,* Terrance passes me a green script. My stomach drops like a water balloon.

"What *is* this?" I ask, trying to give the papers back.

22

"The green revision," Terrance says, handing the boys the same. "Rewritten as of five a.m. I was up all night, so let's just get through this day, everybody."

I scan through it for anything familiar, but everything looks different from the yellow pages I know. When I turn around for my mother, she's at the craft service table slipping granola bars into her purse. She doesn't even eat granola bars. There's half a dozen already in our hotel room.

"Read through it a couple of times together," Terrance says. "Just get used to the changes while I check the camera. Then I'll take you through the blocking."

"So . . . it looks like I start," Jericho says, as if the new script is no big deal. "Okay, cool."

Chris gives the green copy a quick look. Then he nods, ready just like that.

But I'm lost before we even begin. When Doris first sent me the script it was blue. Then when we started shooting it was pink and then yellow. I studied pink for weeks before I had to delete it from my brain. Now I'm ready for yellow. I know yellow. I can do yellow. But *green*?

"Okay . . ." Jericho clears his throat and reads, "I can't believe you're gonna have your own crow's nest. Why didn't we think of this before? This is *genius*."

Chris reads next, as casual and cool as always. "All we'll have to do is climb up here every morning, and we'll be able to see right away how the waves are. No more trekking our boards all the way down to the beach at six in the morning when the water's flat."

"I'm gonna be over here every day!" Jericho says in his raspy voice.

Around me, set decorators are stomping around laying down branches and tools, and production assistants are laughing into their walkie-talkies. Viva is on her phone now, shrugging and talking with her hands.

Jericho nudges me. "Joss, it's your turn . . ."

At school, my teacher gives me "extended time" for tests and quizzes. But on set there's no such thing as "extended time." There's only *now*. I track the page with my finger and search for an easy word that can help me find my place . . .

. . . nest . . .

we . . .

waves . . .

The boys are staring and breathing. I can hear the air through their nostrils. This is worse than school. If I don't say the right words, the boys will find out. Then the crew will find out. Then Terrance will find out.

. . . . .

"What do you like the most about acting?" Terrance asks. His T-shirt is creased from being neatly folded. I bet he's got a closet of these, perfectly stacked.

"Anything at all?" he asks, turning his palms up. "What do you like about being on set?"

"Uh . . ." Finally, I peer up at him—at my favorite kind of face. "Not being at school?"

He laughs with his whole chest. I can't tell if I'm funny to him in a good way or bad, so in a hurry, I think of something to add.

"I mean, I like not having to be me all the time," I say before he counts me out. "I like being somebody else."

"Why?" He leans forward and then away as if he's trying to reel something out of me.

"I don't know," I say. But I do. I've known since the first time I set foot on a set. So I force myself to tell him because I didn't fly all the way to LA for palm trees, and I can tell that he's waiting for some magic words to let him know that I'm really the one. "It's not always fun, I guess . . . to be me."

Terrance isn't laughing now. Instead, he's looking at me as if I really am his sister when she was young and he was young and we're meeting in a time-machine family reunion.

"Listen, Joss. I'm going to film a movie in a studio in Brooklyn and then I'm shooting the rest on Long Island where I grew up. How would you like to visit my hometown?" he asks.

I smile even though I don't know what his hometown is like. "Okay."

"I'll take you to see Montauk Lighthouse."

"Can we climb up it?"

"You bet, kiddo." He taps my leg. "On my set you can do whatever you want."

. . . . .

The words bunch together on the page, one on top of the other. I squint. I hold them close and pull them far. I turn them sideways. But my brain won't straighten them. When I start to shake, so does the script. If people find out, they won't hire me anymore. They'll cast smart girls who can learn on the spot. Everyone is replaceable. Doris says so, even the "next Tatum O'Neal."

"You're here." Jericho points at the name *Norah*.

"I know where I am!" I drop my trembling hands.

"Sorry, I was just trying to help." Jericho raises his eyebrows. "Jeez."

"I don't need help," I snap and stare at Jericho's goofy T-shirt of a hotdog chasing a bun. The shirt isn't from wardrobe. It's his own. He's a stupid-shirt wearer.

Jericho lifts his script. "Great, then let's keep going."

"What are you, the director?" I ask, snottier than I ever thought I could be. It's all I can think of to do. Stall. Pick a fight.

Benji, the production assistant in charge of us kids, is making his way over to us.

"You guys. *Quit it*," Chris says, through his teeth. "Benji's coming."

"Didn't you know, Chris?" I've started something I can't stop. "It's only his first movie, but Jericho's the director now." I sound terrible. I don't want the boys to hate me, Chris especially. But so long as I'm yelling, I'm not rehearsing.

26

"If I *was* the director, I wouldn't let you act like a brat just because you're *Joss Byrd*," Jericho answers, even louder than me.

"Cool it, Jericho. Leave her alone," Chris says. "She's just a little kid."

I'm mad for real now. "I am *not* a little kid!" I yell. I'm not. I'm the most experienced actor here. I'm "wise beyond my years," according to *Entertainment Weekly*. And if anyone's a spoiled brat, it's Jericho. Working, reading, making jokes—everything's easy for him.

"Chill!" Jericho says.

"Hobby actor," I whisper under my breath.

"Kids!" Benji lunges over to us. "Shh . . . Come on. Terrance is right there and so is the producer and so are your parents. I know you don't want me to call them over here."

"Yeah, Jericho," I mumble.

"Yeah, *Joss Byrd*," Jericho mumbles back.

"Stop saying my name like that!" I yell because I'd rather sound bratty than stupid.

"Hey!" Benji holds Jericho and me by the shoulders just as Terrance sprints up the driveway.

"What is going on?" Terrance asks, surprised. I guess the real Norah never shouted like this.

Me and Jericho glare at each other. He squints his eyes into little slits. If I lift my elbow I could clock him in the chin.

"I said no fooling around," Terrance says. "We don't have time for any of this."

I relax back on my heels. Benji lets me go. Then Terrance

waves my mother and Jericho's father over. As I hold my breath, I think of ten different ways my mother might go Viva on me.

"Is something wrong?" Viva walks up with her hand over her phone. She looks from me to Terrance and back again. Her eyes widen when she notices the script in my hands—green.

Terrance touches my mother's arm. "Nothing's wrong, Viva. Nothing's wrong," he says, covering for me. That's the kind of brother Terrance is. "I'd just like you to take Joss to basecamp. I think I want the stunt coordinator to work some more with Rodney and Christopher."

I thank Terrance through mental telepathy. *Thank you, Terrance. I'm sorry for ruining rehearsal. I just didn't want to let you down, not when you picked me to be your very own sister.*

"Joss and Jericho should go to tutoring." Terrance eyes the two of us. "Then I'm sure they'll be ready to shoot this scene after lunch."

"Oh." Viva stares at the script. She clears her throat and clamps her fingers into the back of my neck. "Yes, they definitely will," she says, as if it's so simple. I don't know what I'm doing here. She should've been the actress.

3

"WE'RE CRUNCHED FOR TIME. SO LET'S SEE IF THIS HELPS. Read these over while I make the rest." In my schooling trailer, Viva hands me a batch of index cards with my lines written on them.

"I don't know." I stare at my mother's rushed, sloppy handwriting. "We've never used cards before."

"Well, we're trying it now," she says. "Get your head on straight, and let's do this. I'll read for TJ and Buzz and then you flip to the next card."

I bend the cards in my hands. "But it's just the same lines except on smaller paper," I argue. "What's easier about that?"

"It's less stuff to look at per page!" She smacks the cards with the back of her hand.

"But then how do I know who goes before me or who goes after me? I won't even know who I'm supposed to look at."

"Jesus!" She throws her arms up. "Can't you just work with me here and give it a try, Joss? We don't have forever to argue about it. We'll skip lunch if we have to."

"Hello? Ready for school?" Damon, my tutor, is rattling the door open.

I've never been more relieved to see him. "Yes, I'm ready." I drop the index cards on the counter.

"Good," he says. "I think we have a nice chunk of time to get some work done before lunch."

"One minute, Joss." Viva hands me the script and a marker. "Here. Highlight the rest of your lines while I explain things to Damon."

I slump into my seat. Highlighting is on my list of least favorite things to do.

"We're having sort of a rough morning," Viva tells Damon.

"I'm sorry to hear that." He sets his overstuffed backpack down. Its weight shakes the whole floor. Damon is always ready for action. He tries to bring different things every day, like games or books I'm supposed to like (some have covers of a boy and his dog or kids wearing overalls and playing stickball. *Stickball?*).

"Anything I can help with?" he asks.

"As a matter of fact . . . yes." She glances at me. "You see, Joss and I are in a bit of a bind. But I think that with your help we can get through it."

"How's that?"

"Well, Joss was hired to do a movie, and that's the reason we're all here, isn't it?" she asks, without pausing for his answer. "Good. You've seen her films, right?" When Viva wants to impress someone she calls them films. When she wants to pretend it's no big deal, she calls them movies. "Then you know she can act. But you also know how much she struggles." She glances at me disappointedly. If I had a dollar for every time she looked at me that way I wouldn't have to do this movie in the first place. "Obviously, she's not a reader."

I can sense Damon looking at me while I hide behind my script. He probably agrees that I'm dumb because I can also sense that he's giving me a sad face. I can read people even when I can't see them. I could tell my mother's mood by the back of her head ever since I can remember.

"You mentioned yourself that her schoolwork is already a challenge, and it's only the start of the year," Viva adds.

"She can do it, though," Damon says. "When she's calm and takes her time, she can."

I don't know if Damon means it or if he's just being nice, but it doesn't matter. How can I be calm and take my time on set when all Terrance expects is action?

"Time is exactly the issue," Viva says. "So far we've been able to manage her scenes by running lines every night, but there's a revision."

My mother shows Damon my green script and points out scene 15, but I'm distracted by something going on outside my trailer. Through the window I can see a crowd of noisy kids a couple of years older than me gathering around. A surfer girl, probably an eighth grader, in a striped bikini top and faded cut-off shorts, is balancing an orange surfboard twice her size on her head. "You've been here all week," she says. "How much longer do you expect us to put up with this? This sucks! You can't claim the ocean. You can't claim *nature*." Her tan and her hair that matches wet sand make her look like she was born in the ocean, was raised in it, and is now queen of it.

I'll get to surf for our last scene of *The Locals*. I've never surfed before. I hope I can look half as cool as this girl. I also hope I can stay as flat as she is when I'm her age. Her chest is as flat as her board.

The surfer girl's scabby, blond-streaked friends start pounding their boards on the ground. They're gonna start either a song or a war.

"Yeah! This is a public beach!"

"This is bootleg!"

"The ocean is our temple, man!"

They must be the locals—the *real* locals.

There are postings along the beach that say something like, *Due to film production on these dates, there will be no surfing between the orange signs.* Like a pop-up city, our production has taken over the entire beach parking lot and turned it into our production basecamp. At basecamp we have our dressing trailers back-to-back; we can hear each other's TVs and toilets. One time I heard Chris sing "Happy Birthday" to his mother on the phone, which made me want to hug him through the wall. I also heard Rodney hacking up a loogie and spitting it into the sink, which made me want to barf. Wardrobe and the hair and makeup trucks are parked in an L-shape. This way, we can walk quickly from one to the next. The production offices are in trailers, too, including Terrance's office and Peter Bustamante's. Their doors say Director and Executive Producer. There's trucks for the cameras and others for lighting and all our gear. (I don't know what all the rolls of glow tape and switchboards and steel poles are for, but trust me: in the end they make a movie.) By the surfer kids' faces, it's obvious that us taking over their beach at the end of September isn't making us very popular in town.

"Here's how this is going to happen," my mother says. "I know you have to report her schoolwork to her teachers. But what I'll do is, I'm just gonna sign off on all of her assignments." She pretends to sign her name in the air. "That way you don't have to worry about your paperwork. And on your end, you're gonna help Joss learn her lines."

The last time I was in school my class was working on persuasive arguments. One of the strategies is that you're supposed to point out the advantages for the other person even when you're looking to get something for yourself. My mother would've gotten an A.

"I trust you'll keep this to yourself, for life or longer." She lowers her voice, for nobody's sake.

Me and my mother are pros at keeping my school problems to ourselves. Doris doesn't even know. We want to stay at the very top of her client list. The last thing we need is for her to peg me as some sort of problem.

"Uh, Mrs. Byrd . . ."

"*Ms.* And please, call me Viva, already."

"Viva, I appreciate the challenge you're up against here. It must be an enormous pressure to make a movie. I'm sure. But I'm an educator. And I'm required to cover three hours of academics a day." He pats the textbooks on the table. "Anyway, I'm not an acting coach. I don't know anything about movies. I just graduated from college. I took this job to teach actual subjects. Sixth grade is a lot more demanding than fifth. Joss has a unit on geometry, and she has the Egyptians to study, and homework for English—"

"A Terrance James Rivenbach autobiographical screenplay is English. Joss needs this more than she needs *Are You There God? It's Me, Margaret.*"

Teachers are always busting my butt to read that. They think if any book will get me reading, that might be the one. Good thing I never spent the effort since Viva doesn't even think it's worth it.

My mother doesn't want to fire Damon. She likes him and so do I. I liked my tutor from my last job, too. She used to boil down my chapters to the bare bones and only make me answer the important questions. I requested her again, but she works on a TV series now, so I didn't know who was going to walk through the door this time. I was worried I might get someone real strict. But me and Damon get along. He's young, his hair is spiky, plus, he's Asian. I know that doesn't automatically make a person smart and hardworking, but for him it's true.

34

"I'm sure there's still room for schoolwork," Damon says.

"No. No." Viva shakes her head, getting down to business. No more *Ms.* Nice Girl. "Look, you're a crew member here. This is how it works on set. You're part of production. That means we all share the same goal, which is to make this movie." Another strategy of persuasive arguments is to present the facts.

Damon inspects the script and flips the pages. "I'm really happy to be part of the crew, Ms. Byrd, uh, Viva. But I'm a teacher. I don't think the movie should be *my* goal."

Outside, the surfer girl is raising her voice at our crew about her rights as a "resident of Montauk and a citizen of the U.S.A." I like all her bracelets. Maybe I can get some just like them as soon as we wrap; they're rubber or rope or twisted strands of colored cloth. She's lifting one foot now to scratch her heel with her big toe. Her bony hips jut out above her shorts. I wonder how the waves don't snap her in half.

"Kids go to school to figure out what they're going to be, right?" This is the clincher. Viva is getting to her most logical point.

"Well, that's part of it—"

"Let's face it. Joss isn't gonna be a lawyer or an accountant or a doctor or anything. Luckily, she's already doing what she's gonna be. So let's get on board here." She waves her arm to welcome Damon aboard.

I might be behind in school, but I'm ahead in life. That's what my mother always tells me. But it doesn't feel that way when she lists everything I'm not going to be. Hiding behind my script, I scan for *Norah* on page 68. One of my parts is, like, ten sentences long.

"Her school in Tyrone . . ." Viva sighs. "All they want to do is test her some more so that they can slap an official label on her. But Joss doesn't need a label, Damon. She needs a career. Joss is an actress, not a dyslexic."

"Your movie sucks balls!" the surfer girl yells. Then she turns with her board on her head and screams, "Hairy balls!" She walks ahead of the group by a good five steps, with the leash from her surfboard dragging along the ground. Now *that* girl is ahead in life.

Damon shakes his head. "But a label could help. Maybe Joss would get the support she needs."

"Or it could give people a reason not to cast her," Viva says. "We're not taking that chance. We just have to work harder than everyone else. You're not afraid to work hard, are you?"

"Of course not, Viva," Damon says. "But I'm not sure if this is the—"

"Damon, Joss will do whatever it takes. But she just needs you to get her through it. Show him, Joss."

They both stare at me like I'm a monkey in a lab.

I turn my head from the window. "Huh?" I didn't expect this part of the persuasive argument: the demonstration.

"Read a little for him," Viva says. I hate her for putting me on the spot. But this is the deal I made. I promised she wouldn't have to force me to do the work again.

"That's not necessary, Viva," Damon says kindly. "She reads for me every day. Don't you, Joss?"

"No, no," my mother insists. "You should see what a colossal embarrassment this shoot is going to be if you don't help us. Joss, go ahead." It's like she's asking the monkey to point from ball to block to banana.

I clear my throat to read because I was the one who made Viva turn the truck around. And as embarrassing as it is, I also know that this will get Damon to help me because as soon as I look at the page, the letters will start to float and the words will mash one on top of the other.

But before I start, I look out the window again. The surfer girl, who's leading her pack out of the parking lot, does two things at once that I can only dream of doing: she balances her board on her head with one hand, and with her other hand, she flips our movie crew the finger.

. . . . .

"I'm never going to learn the new lines by lunchtime. I'll look like an idiot." I sulk over the back of my chair and watch Damon as he reads through the new pages. "My mother's gonna kill me," I say, even though I'm afraid of so much more, like the whole world finding out that I'm a phony.

"Hang on, now. Nobody's killing anybody," Damon says. "Where's the old script—the yellow?"

"Why?"

"I just want to check something."

I pull the yellow script from my backpack.

Damon opens both versions in front of him on the sofa. "I knew it!" He brings me both copies and sets them on the table. "The dialogue is the same. It's just switched around."

"So?"

"So, that means you already know the words. All you have to do is learn them in a different order," he says, as if it's easy. "For example, Chris used to have the first line. But now Jericho does. Then it's Chris and then Jericho again. You just have to respond to Jericho instead."

"Whaaat?" I ask. How can I learn the actual lines when I can't even understand this much?

"Don't get frustrated. We haven't even read it through yet."

"But this scene is supposed to be snappy. The boys talk so fast, and I'm used to the old version." I hold my head. I can practically hear Jericho mocking me again: *Joss Byrd.*

"Okay, take a breather." Damon sits quietly and lets me mope. After a few minutes, he opens his laptop and taps the keys. "Maybe we should take a step back and explore our options, okay?"

"Yes, *please*," I beg.

When I look outside, I see that the surfer kids have gone, but there's a woman in a baseball cap and surf shorts pacing and talking on her phone. Something about her square face and her tight lips looks familiar. Maybe she just reminds me of someone on TV. She must be stressed. I can tell by the way she's holding her neck and trying to get the kinks out. She's probably a surfer. We probably ruined her day off. Whatever her problem is, she should get over it because I bet I'm having a worse day than she is.

"Acting class . . . acting class . . ." Damon types the search words and then scans through the videos. "Donna Joy Carena's School of Acting . . . Acting Class for Beginners . . . Acting Class Fails . . ."

"Donna Joy Carena, let's see what you've got." Damon hits play.

Donna Joy has dandelions in her hair and bare feet. Her face is eighty but her frilly dress is for someone who's eight. "Imagine becoming your favorite flower. You're stretching, you're opening and opening and opening up toward the sun . . ." Donna Joy Carena stretches both arms toward the sky.

"No way," I say. "I'm not being my favorite flower."

"Agreed." Damon scrolls down the choices. He clicks on one video of a girl standing on a chair holding a script. The girl delivers one line and loses her balance. The chair tips, she falls onto the stage then slides into the orchestra pit. Damon laughs. "Sorry. Not what we're looking for . . . pretty funny, though."

This is a slippery slope. Me and Viva can watch videos of fat cats in sinks or tours of celebrity dream closets for hours and hours. We'll start after lunch on a Sunday afternoon and the next thing we know it's dark and time for dinner.

Damon clicks the arrow to the next page. "Yale Drama School?"

Yale sounds hard. "Nah."

"Meryl Streep went there."

I can't remember who that is.

"No. You're right. Too snooty. I went to Fordham. Much more down-to-earth."

Fordham sounds hard, too. I knew Damon was smart.

"You should've taught regular school," I say. He would've been happier teaching all those subjects to smart kids.

"I will, eventually," he says, scrolling down the screen. "But I thought this'd be a good adventure." Damon stops at a video called "Nailing the Scene with Vern LaVeque." He looks at me hopefully. "Vern LaVeque? That name sounds like he knows what he's talking about, right?"

"I guess." We are the blind leading the blind, as Terrance says when his crew can't seem to get their act together.

At the same time, me and Damon check the clock on the microwave. Two hours to go until lunch.

"Uh . . . we can skip part one, right?" Damon says. "You've already been in real movies."

"Okay."

He presses play for part two.

In front of a cheesy hand-painted mural of the ocean stands Vern LaVeque in a too-tight black T-shirt and an orange tan.

"So, the key to everything I've been saying is that the lines are not what matter in a scene!" Vern LaVeque raises his arms above his students. "Let go of the lines. And let go of the fear!"

I sit taller and lean toward the screen. I thought I was the only one who felt any fear.

"The key to an effective scene is not reading! It is NOT READING! It's LISTENING!"

"Score." Damon turns over a piece of paper and picks up a pencil.

"So you better believe me when I say this because it is the plain truth. If you can listen"—Vern LaVeque points to his ears. Then he points to his body—"then you can act!"

Me and Damon smile at each other.

"You're a good listener, aren't you?" Damon asks.

"I listen all the time," I say. Even when I don't want to hear stuff, like Viva calling this shoot a potential colossal embarrassment, I'm still listening.

On his paper, Damon writes:

~~READING~~ → LISTENING.

Vern LaVeque struts across the carpeted stage and points to his students. The veins on his arms rise as he flexes. "You know the words. You've been up to here with the words!" He holds his hand to his forehead.

"Tell me about it," I say.

"So I want you to throw that script aside!" Vern LaVeque flings a script off his stool. The pages flap in the air and land on the floor like a lame bird. "You've gone over the lines inside

41

and out. Trust that they're in here." He points to his head. "Trust that you have them and focus on your partner. I want you to listen to your scene partner. Listen to him so carefully that you hear every word and every breath."

I think about Chris. When he's excited his voice crackles at the end of his sentences, and when he's upset he sighs real loudly before he speaks. I like listening to Chris.

"Listen to your partner, and allow his words to trigger your heart, your character's heart." Vern LaVeque clutches his chest dramatically. "Tap into your character's emotions and use them."

LISTEN → HEART, Damon writes.

I'm good with emotions. The *Hollywood Reporter* called me "fiercely emotional." They said I had "complete conviction." And Chris, if I'm being honest, already triggers my heart.

"I'm tapped into my emotions," I say softly.

"Yeah, you are!" Damon grins at me.

On the screen, Vern LaVeque looks into the camera like he's talking straight to me. "Feel like your character. And allow your heart to trigger the right words."

"Does that make sense to you?" Damon asks.

"I should listen closely to the boys. Then I'll feel how Norah would feel. And my heart will remind me what my line is," I say. "So it doesn't matter if the dialogue is in a different order!"

"You got it. That's exactly what he's saying." Damon and I high-five.

"So, what's the secret?" Vern LaVeque asks.

"Listening!" his students answer.

"Listening," I repeat in my full voice.

"That's right. LISTEN! Listen to your partner." He points to people in the class. "Listen to what is happening around you. Listen and feel and react. Because acting is *re*acting."

LISTEN → FEEL → REACT, Damon writes.

"Reacting!" I shout. "Acting is *re*acting!"

Vern LaVeque points from student to student. He stops, holds his chest, and lowers his head. "LISTEN to your character's HEART, and the words will come."

"Listen to Norah's heart . . ." I close my eyes as if I'm praying. In a way, I am praying for this to work. ". . . and the words will come."

"That, my friends," Vern LaVeque says, "is what nailing the scene is about."

"Please work. Please, please, please work." I point from my ears to my heart to my mouth.

4

IF THE LOCALS HATE US FOR TAKING OVER THEIR "TEMPLE," they probably can't stand that we eat lunch in their real church basement. Whenever we're down here I never remember we're even in a church. There're the usual statues: Mary in a half shell and Joseph (I think) and apostles (I've seen Jesus movies at Easter time). But none of us pay any attention because we're too hungry to feel holy. I've only felt holy once. Viva took me to church when her friend's baby got baptized. Even when the babies started to cry I couldn't believe how peaceful it was in there. I wouldn't mind going to church again, just to be able to sit with my mother for an hour in quiet.

Our caterers, Lights, Catering, Action!, cook up all of our food inside their catering truck. Then they set up a buffet lunch as if we're at a wedding or something. The chef gets lots of complaints about too much salt or overcooked this or undercooked that. But I don't know what all the moaning is about because at home a home-cooked meal is fish sticks and toast with ketchup packets we collect from McDonald's. Here the buffet's got a beef station, a seafood station, cold pasta, hot pasta, four salads to choose from, a dozen dressings, chicken and mushrooms, roasted vegetables, paella, and something that looks like beef stew but isn't, but I'm sure it's good, too. If you ask me, the food truck is the greatest thing Hollywood ever created, besides *Paper Moon*. Seriously, how does all of *this* come out of *that*?

I don't get how so many actresses can be anorexic, especially when catering has a ravioli station on Fridays: there's cheese ravioli, mushroom ravioli, and lobster ravioli with a choice of sauces. What I get is marinara on the cheese ravioli, cream on the mushroom ravioli, and butter and garlic on the lobster ravioli. But that's on Fridays. Today is a rice pudding day. Finally, something's going my way. Rice pudding is a universal favorite. The strategy is to take your share of pudding before you line up for the real food because if you wait until after, there might not be any left.

"Joss!" Chris calls my name and rushes up behind me as I'm loading three little pudding cups on my tray. Why don't they just put the pudding in bigger cups? "I gotta talk to you," he says, no nonsense.

"I'll know the lines after lunch, okay?" I slice him like a paper cut. "Don't I *always* know the lines when we shoot?"

"What?" He crinkles his forehead. "No, no. It's not about that. I don't care about that," he says, taking four pudding cups for himself.

If this isn't about rehearsal, I don't know what it could be. I shouldn't have been so rude. I'm still touchy about the script, that's all.

"Ah! Rice pudding day!" Terrance calls from the back of the line. "No hoarding, ladies and gentlemen! One per customer!" he jokes, pointing at Chris. "I see you, Christopher Tate! That is a direct violation of catering code 421, section B!"

"Just get your food, and sit with me out back, okay?" Chris says, walking toward the back door.

"Okay." I try not to look surprised, but I am. We never eat together, just the two of us. Sometimes Chris eats with Jericho, to talk about how to get to the next level on a video game or to quote some TV show I've never heard of.

I thought it'd be easy to make friends with other kids who act. But it isn't, not when they think I'm Miss Thing when I'm not. When we got to Long Island, Chris asked if I wanted to go to Splish-Splash water park with him and Jericho. I wanted to go so bad. They were all excited about the Giant Twister—three slides that twist through the trees and end up in one pool. The three of us could've gone down at the same time. But, like a complete snob, I told them I didn't want to go because water parks are where you get pink eye and foot fungus. How could I tell Chris that I had to stay in to memorize lines because I'm dense? I couldn't.

. . . . .

46

Jericho and Chris barrel into my schoolroom at our Brooklyn studio. They thump their heavy backpacks onto the table where I'm showing Damon this year's textbooks. Soon enough Damon will find out that books are not my claim to fame.

"Ding, ding! School's in!" Jericho says.

"Whoa, wait a second, guys!" Damon holds up a hand. "This isn't school for you."

I'm supposed to tutor alone. Viva told the producer that she wants me to have the best possible education. But really, me and my mother just don't want anyone to find out how slow I am.

"But Benji sent us," Chris says. "We're supposed to start tutoring today."

"It says school on the door!" Jericho points at the sign.

"Sorry. Not with me. You two have another teacher," Damon says. "I only have Joss."

"Your schoolroom is at the end of the hallway," I add. "The door says TJ & BUZZ'S SCHOOL."

"Oh . . ." Chris says. "Okay." He and Jericho pick up their things and leave.

It would be so cool if I could tutor with them. It's boring to do school alone day after day. But I don't want them to know my problems any more than Viva does.

"Why does she get her own private tutor?" I hear Jericho ask as they shuffle down the hall.

"I don't know," Chris says. "Probably because she's a big deal."

. . . . .

"Hey, sit here." Chris says, meaning with him on the back steps.

I might be blushing. I know it's messed up to blush over a boy who's supposed to be my brother, but usually when I'm alone with Chris we're playing Norah and TJ. When I'm not acting, I can't help it.

We set our trays between us, and I wait for Chris to speak.

"Man, that rehearsal . . ." He rubs his dirty forehead. "I practiced the fight with Rodney."

I listen quietly and watch some bees buzzing over a garbage can.

"The stunt coordinator showed Rodney how to smack me and shove me and yell in my face," he says, shoulders slumped.

For once I'm grateful to my mother. No yelling in my face or smacking or shoving for me. Chris has it tough. The movie wouldn't work without rough scenes between him and Rodney. There's no way around violent content for Chris.

"At one point he rubs my head into the dirt." Chris takes a deep breath and pushes his salad around with a knife. (He eats a lot of salad for a boy.) "There's a way to do it so it's not real-real. But man, oh man . . . it's *kind* of real. I mean, if I'm on the ground I'm on the ground, right?"

I want to wipe the dirt off his cheek, but I don't dare. If I was pretty and fourteen and he thought of me as a girl instead of a "little kid," as he called me, I would. But I'm not, and he doesn't, so I won't. This could've been one of those movie moments:

48

boy needs comforting. Girl is the only one who understands. Close up on both. His eyes. Her eyes. They lean closer. Will they kiss or won't they? But really it's just Christopher Tate and me sitting next to some bees at a stinking garbage can.

"Does it hurt?" I ask.

"It doesn't tickle, I'll tell you that. And of course we're going to have to do it, like, fifty times from every angle."

He's right. It might take all day to get it right. In my last movie, a fight scene took four hours.

"It'd be fine if Rodney would maybe, like, joke around or something with me at least. But he's always *in* it; he's always in the zone. It feels like he hates me in real life."

Rodney's stare through the screen door was mean enough for me. I can't imagine a punch, even a fake one.

"Why'd I ever say I would do this? I'm missing the first month of high school." He kicks a pebble that hits the garbage can square in the middle. "Last week was soccer tryouts. They'll never let me on now." Chris stabs a tomato slice, leaving the knife sticking straight up.

Right now I don't know what's harder: being an actor who hates school or being an actor who likes it. But me and Chris are one and the same in a bigger way; he needs to work. His folks and older brothers run a restaurant in Florida. I don't think it does very good.

"What if the only reason I was cast is because I look like Terrance in that picture?" Chris asks.

I don't know what to say. I've been wanting to bond more with Chris, but I was imagining spending a day at Dave & Buster's arcade.

"I've never done a drama before," Chris says. "Just comedies—stupid stuff, like riding a Razor scooter through the hallways and junk."

I've seen the movie he means—*Sixth Period Lunch*—but I don't say so because I've seen it more times than I want to admit. And when I found out we were going to work together I watched all of his scenes again.

Chris holds his head and lets out a loud sigh. "Ugh . . . I'm supposed to cry, too."

That's one part of the script that always stays the same: *TJ cries.* He's almost crying now. *Just hold on to that,* I want to tell him, but I don't want to interrupt the thoughts that are swirling around in his mind.

"I've seen *Hit the Road* and *Buy One, Get One,*" he says, finally looking at me.

I stare at my rice. It doesn't affect me much when a hundred strangers watch my work, but I care what Chris thinks. Chris seeing my movies is kind of like him reading my diary, if I had a diary. I look so young in those movies. No wonder he thinks of me as a kid.

"I've seen you cry and scream and all that on-screen." He leans forward as if I've got the key to the universe. "How do you do that?"

In *Sixth Period Lunch*, Chris Razor scootered through the cafeteria, smiling at the girls. In this one part, he takes off his hat and puts it on the prettiest girl as he glides past her. I can't believe a boy like that wants advice from *me*. I just learned that acting is reacting from YouTube, so what do I even know?

"Well, uh . . ." I pick the dirt under my fingernails while I think about how to describe what I do. "I use my triggers."

"What are triggers?"

I peek at Chris. He's serious. He really wants my help. "Uh . . . they're bad stuff from my life," I say quietly.

He nods for me to go on. He doesn't care what my triggers are. He only wants to know how I use them, so I sit taller and explain.

"I ask for quiet fifteen minutes before a tough scene, block everything else out, and think about it real hard until I feel it behind my eyes and my face and in my throat." I hold my neck as I speak. "And then I bust it all out the second I hear 'Action.'"

Chris sits real quiet for a long time, biting the inside of his mouth. It's probably the dumbest thing he's ever heard, and he's wondering why he bothered asking me. He should ask Rodney how to get in the zone.

Chris laughs. "I think I'm going to need more than fifteen minutes."

I laugh with him. "Well, like the way you're feeling now. If you can bottle it up, then you can use it later."

"Oh, great." He throws up his hands. "I don't feel so bad anymore."

"You can get yourself worked up again," I say, secretly happy that I've made him feel better. "Use a trigger. Really. The more you practice doing it, the faster it works."

He gives me a slight smile. "Okay. It's worth a shot."

We pick up our trays and head back inside. The basement is filled up now with our starved crew, and just as I predicted, the rice pudding cups are gone. But there's some saint statue standing behind the dessert table with his arms open, praying for more.

We pass Rodney filling his tray. I can feel him watching me when I cross the room; it gives me the creeps. Poor Chris.

"Too hot outside?" Terrance asks as me and Chris join the table with the rest of the group.

"Bees," I say.

"Yeah. Swarms," Chris adds, and I feel like we're in on something together.

"Well, be careful. If you get bit on the face, that'll be it," Viva says. She's very into protecting my face, not for my safety, but for the camera.

"Not bit. *Stung*," I say.

"Cool it, Smart-mouth," she says, giving me the eye. "And cover your wardrobe." She tucks my napkin into my collar and spreads it across my chest as if I'm a baby about to eat mashed carrots. My wardrobe is a tank top with a picture of a rocket ship on the front. It's already dirtied on purpose, but it's not supposed to get dirty by mistake.

Just as we're getting settled, Rodney reaches across the table and snatches two of Chris's rice pudding cups as he heads to his seat. The grown-ups ignore it, but Chris closes his eyes and curses under his breath. I feel so bad that I give him one of my puddings as soon as Rodney turns his back. Let me tell you, pudding is the last thing that Rodney needs. He's plenty mushy around the middle, and don't even try to tell me he put on those pounds for his character.

"I got some extra potato salad. I know how much you like it, TJ." My mother passes Terrance the bowl. She started using his nickname when we first got to the studio in Brooklyn. She likes getting chummy with people from the start. But I'd feel disrespectful calling him TJ.

"Ah, thank you. Bonus," he says, mixing the potatoes with his corn. He passes me another napkin, since mine is around my neck. I grin at him. Terrance says that having meals together makes for a better movie because it makes us feel sort of like we're a family. He's right. This is the type of family I'd like, anyway.

The closest I ever had to a dad was Brian Shea Towson; he played my country singer dad in *Hit the Road*. We ate all our lunches together, too. I liked calling him Pops, even off set, which I guess is kind of like staying in character.

"Go easy there with the healthy stuff, Joss. What is that,

broccoli?" Terrance inspects my tray. "If you get too tall, we'll have to recast you."

Not funny. And there goes a perfectly nice lunch with my happy imaginary family. I stare at my buttered roll.

If I could stunt my growth so I could play a child forever, believe me, I would. I'm lucky I still look young enough to play Norah. Doris says that being small in Hollywood is the pot of gold. There're a ton of parts until the awkward age. I'm living proof of that because I keep playing younger than I am. In *The Locals*, Norah is meant to be ten even though I'm twelve.

Terrance is talking to Christopher now, about the real day he tried to build the crow's nest. "I want you to remember the excitement I felt at the beginning. That lookout was going to be my connection to the ocean, the one place I really loved. It was going to be my escape."

Chris is pushing his food around as he listens. He's under a lot of pressure, but at least he gets to talk with Terrance about his part. I don't know how Norah felt about the crow's nest or the ocean, and I don't know what's really in her heart. I've never played a real person before. I wish I could talk to her and know that I'm doing good enough.

"Terrance, when am I gonna meet the real Norah? You mailed my letter, right?" I say. Norah lives somewhere nearby. Damon helped me write a quick note asking her to visit the set. Terrance gave me her address to put on it.

"Don't be pushy, Joss," my mother says. "Sorry." She squeezes Terrance's arm and leaves her hand there.

"It's fine." Terrance winks at me. "I did mail it, kiddo. I'd love for Norah to come. But she's very busy, my sister. She must be out of town." Terrance drops his fork into his not-beef-stew and then he pokes me on the nose. I don't mind if he treats me like I'm ten when we're on set. But I wish he wouldn't do that in real life, especially in front of Chris. "But she's very proud of her mini-self. She really is."

"Well . . . okay," I say.

Just then I notice a plastic wristband on Terrance's arm. Chris is wearing one, too. "Hey, what are those wristbands?" I ask.

"Chris and I went to the driving range last night."

"We got unlimited refills—golf balls, not sodas," Chris says.

"Oh." Besides missing so many good times, another problem with turning down invitations is that after a while you stop getting invited altogether. "Then what about the lighthouse?" I ask Terrance. "When can you take me?"

"Joss, TJ has enough to do right now. Don't go bugging him about sightseeing," my mother says, even though Terrance had time for the driving range and the lighthouse was his idea in the first place. If Viva would stop kissing up to Terrance for two seconds, it'd be two seconds of pigs flying.

"But we're supposed to take trick pictures that look like I'm holding the lighthouse in my palm. Terrance said he'd do them with me."

"Let's all nail scene fifteen first." Terrance isn't kidding even a little. "Then we'll talk lighthouse. And Chris, don't forget to cut the wristband off before the shoot."

55

Chris is biting the inside of his mouth again. I can tell that Terrance is making him even more nervous, so I drop my napkin on the floor and pull him down with me.

"You know," I whisper under the table. "They can give you tear drops."

"They can?" he asks, surprised.

"Sure." I cover my full mouth. "The makeup department's got tears in a dropper. Plenty of actors use them."

His face lights up. "Do you use them?"

"No . . ." I feel bad about that, for some reason. He looks so worried that I almost tell him I've been studying Vern LaVeque's Master Class. Almost. "I don't use them, but *everybody* does," I say instead. "No one cares, anyway. No one cares how you get the shot, as long as you get it." That sounds like something Viva would say, but it isn't. That line is all me.

5

CAROLINE, MY STAND-IN, IS TWENTY-THREE BUT MY HEIGHT
and my coloring. We each get a stand-in: Jericho and Chris get
Warner and Davey (grown-ups who are small). And Rodney gets
a big guy named Frosty who's as doughy as him. Our stand-ins
pretend to be us so that the crew can set up the camera and the
lights and practice shooting all the movement without us. That's
how we get time to rest or tutor, or in Rodney's case, to order
fast food and nap in his trailer.

I'm obsessed with stand-ins; on *Hit the Road* I couldn't
believe that I got one. For some reason I thought stand-ins
would be only for adults. But that's how come I realized I was
an actor, too. I figured if I needed a backup, I must be somebody important.

I wish I had a stand-in for real life. Can you imagine having
someone walk through your day to make sure everything's fine
before it's your turn? She could warn me, "Watch out for Viva.
She's snippy today!" or "There's a pop quiz on fractions. Number
3 is C!" I could get used to that.

Caroline is up in my tree when we get back to set after lunch. She waves to me on my way inside the house. Viva says that stand-ins do a lot of work but don't get any glory. Caroline told me she likes this gig but is trying to get a real acting job. But to me, being a stand-in should come under the heading of count your blessings because she gets to stay at the Beachcomber, too, and she gets to eat all the same catering and sit up in a tree for the day. Best of all, she never has to learn any lines. If you ask me, she's pretty much got it made. So, I guess it all depends on your definition of *glory*.

Basecamp is too far away from set for us to get shuttled back and forth between takes, and we finished filming interior shots at the soundstage, so Damon and me are going to tutor in the house during the backyard scene. I'm supposed to do school for fifteen hours a week. Benji keeps track of my hours in a leather memo pad as if his life depends on it. He says that production can get in trouble if I don't meet my schooling requirements. We're two hours behind from last week, so that adds up to needing seventeen hours for this week. But Damon said we should try to live in the present. In other words, we're in denial about having to make it all up in the end just like we're in denial about the reading he wants me to do, and the long list of classwork Viva will sign off on. I've brought my backpack with some books, but they're just for appearances. All we're really going to do here is practice Vern LaVeque's listening, feeling, and reacting. Denial is just a real-life type of acting.

The inside of this house is worse than the outside. The floor-boards squeak, and the whole place smells like old people.

"Hey, how are you? Kind of a spooky house, isn't it?" Damon says to Rodney as we pass each other in the tight hallway, but all Damon gets back is a cold stare. This house isn't the only thing that's scary.

I think it's rude to be in character with people who aren't even in the movie. If you have to practice your part 24/7, then maybe you aren't that good of an actor. I'm no Meryl Streep (I remembered who she is. She's won *three* Oscars), but fifteen minutes is always plenty of time for me.

This house must be between getting sold and either being bought or knocked down by a wrecking ball because there isn't any furniture in it. There's a fold-up table and a couple of chairs set up for us in one of the upstairs bedrooms. The windows are already open, but it's still stuffy. I wouldn't be surprised if the old folks who lived here died of suffocation right here in this room. It's a good thing I don't believe in ghosts because this house would be haunted, for sure.

"I'll go see if they can get us a fan. And I'll bring us up some waters," Damon says. "Then we'll practice 'Nailing the Scene with Vern LaVeque.' But you have to do some schoolwork later, okay?"

"Okay," I answer. That's fair enough. I guess denial can only last for so long.

"Do you want anything else from downstairs?"

"No, thank you."

I hear him say "Excuse me" to someone on the staircase—someone with very heavy feet.

Those footsteps come closer to my room. They stop. They start again.

"Are you doing school up here?" It's Rodney in the doorway. He must be bored. He must be giving himself a tour. Sometimes there's no place to hang out on set. The trailers can't come with us when the streets are tight.

"Yes."

Rodney steps in without being invited. His body practically fills the whole room. He's breathing hard; the stairs must've taken a lot out of him. "It's nice and quiet up here," he says slowly, without blinking.

This is the first time he's ever spoken to me. I don't like it. I want to tell him that no one's allowed in the schoolroom. That's an actual child labor law. My last tutor said so; she was very into following laws. But I'm not as tough as the mouthy surfer girl from the parking lot. I don't ask Rodney to leave.

He moves in closer. The stains on his undershirt from wardrobe are meant to be grease and beer. But I'll bet his real T-shirts are exactly like it. I notice chest hair through a hole, so I turn away. He's disgusting.

He leans over me, smelling of sweat and onions and cigarettes. "What are you learning?"

"Nothin'." I look down at my script. "I'm just going over the dialogue."

"Oh, yeah?" He pushes the yellowed curtain aside and peeks out the window. "Where's your punk brother?"

"He's supposed to be tutoring in the kitchen," I say coldly. And then, imagining the tough surfer girl's tangled bracelets on my own arm, I add, "And he's not my real brother. It's just a *movie*."

"What a little bastard, that kid," he says, unchanged.

"Chris is cool," I say, sure to use Chris's real name. "He works hard. He wants to do a good job."

Rodney looks out the window again and then toward the staircase. "Where'd your tutor go?"

"He went to get us a fan."

"Good." Rodney stands behind me and presses himself right up against the back of my chair until it creaks. His body heat rises against my back. "It's pretty hot up here."

"Uh-huh." I squirm and turn a page of my script. I don't even know if I'm on the right scene. "He'll be right back."

I can see Rodney's reflection in the window. With his wide chest looming over me, he lifts his meaty hands and lowers them onto my bare shoulders. His skin is touching my skin.

"I gotta go," I blurt, slipping out from under his fingers. I run past him out of the room and speed down the stairs and through the front door.

"Hey, wait! Get back up here!"

"Whoa! Be careful!" somebody shouts.

I think that I'm hyperventilating. I've never hyperventilated before, so I'm not sure if this is it, but I think so. On TV I've seen people breathe into a paper bag, but all I've got are my own hands, so I cup them around my mouth and try to breathe my own air back in. I keep at it—deep breath in and deep breath out—until I stop shaking. I wipe my shoulders off, thinking of those giant sausage fingers touching me.

When I look up, there're groups of locals on the sidewalk and in the street trying to get a glimpse of the shoot in the backyard. They're pulling out their phones, so I straighten up against the wooden post and force myself to look normal.

Nothing happened . . . nothing happened . . . nothing happened . . . I tell myself. *He's just in character. He's only rehearsing, just like Terrance said. He's in the zone, the same as he was with Chris. It was just like him taking pudding cups. That's all.*

A couple of teenagers are waving. I smile and give a hello as they take my picture. Doing this makes me feel better, as if nothing happened, which it didn't. Because Rodney was only pretending. *Nothing more, nothing less.*

Farther down the block there's one lady standing alone. I remember her from this morning. She's the grown-up surfer I saw on the phone back at basecamp.

"Hey, Joss?" Benji calls from inside. "You have to get back to school. Try to get twenty minutes in before Terrance calls you. We got you a fan. I'm going to start your school clock as soon as you get back inside."

I stare at the lady. There's something so familiar about her; now I'm sure it's not just a TV resemblance.

"In a sec, Benji!" I answer. "I just need some air."

The woman is pinching her elbow and standing with her legs apart. When she takes her hat off to fix her ponytail, I notice that her hair and her skin are the same exact color as mine.

I run toward her. "Norah! I knew it! I knew you'd come! Norah? It's me. I'm Joss!"

She stares at me, shocked.

"I'm Joss Byrd!" I hop up and down in front of her. "I'm playing *you*! I'm TJ's sister!"

Her face drops. Long bangs fall over her eyes.

"You're Norah, aren't you?" I ask, even though I'm positive it's her. "Didn't you come to see me? Didn't you get my letter?"

Terrance is coming up to us now, waving me back to the house. "Joss! Joss, no! Let her be."

"You don't want to be me." Norah says, looking angrily over my shoulder at Terrance. "And you don't want to be TJ's sister. You don't even want to know him." She turns and walks away.

"But I—" I want to talk with her the way Chris talks with Terrance, and I want her to be proud of me. I take a few steps to follow her.

"Leave her, kiddo."

"Terrance?" I turn to him, confused. "Why is she mad at me?"

"Drop it, Joss." He leads me up the driveway beside the speedboat that's parked in dried mud.

"She hates me, doesn't she?" I say. She must've wanted a

prettier girl, a real actor—somebody glamorous. Maybe *I* was only cast because I look like her in that old picture.

"She hates a lot of things, Joss. But this is nothing you need to worry about. I told her to stay away. She never should've showed up here."

I thought he wanted Norah to visit me. "But you told me—"

Terrance grabs my arms. "I need you right here, okay?" He points two fingers at his face.

"Why would she say that?" I ask, still staring after Norah.

"Look here. Look at me." He lowers to one knee. "Listen. *You're* Norah now, okay? *You. Not* her. Say it. Say, '*I'm* Norah.'"

I concentrate on Terrance's eyes—still my favorite kind of face. I want to trust him. He's my director. He picked me for a reason. He won't let me fail. I want so bad to believe that I'm good enough.

"*I'm* Norah."

"Again." He shakes me lightly.

"*I'm* Norah now."

"Good." As he lets me go I notice Rodney watching us from behind the house.

"Joss! Focus. The camera is almost ready for you," Terrance says, all business. "And Caroline looks happy as a clam up in that tree, doesn't she?"

Now I'm angry at Caroline. If she were my real-life stand-in she could've warned me about this afternoon. And then I would've steered clear of Rodney, and I would know why Norah hates me and what I should do about it.

"Peter Bustamante's here. It's not every day that the producer gets to see you work. And Christopher's been pushing so hard in rehearsal. This is his big moment. You want to help him through it, don't you?"

I think that I'm nodding. I don't know; I'm so confused.

"Wait till you see him. He's gonna be gangbusters. He told me you two talked the scene over. I'm so proud of you both. You're such a good team." Terrance places his palm on my head for a few seconds. "Pull yourself into the scene, okay?"

The set is waiting for us. The camera is pointing up at the tree. That means the opening shot of scene 15 will be on me—the unworthy Norah. A white screen is bouncing sunlight up into the leaves. Caroline is sitting on the fattest branch. Whistling and swinging her leg and looking up at an airplane flying by, she looks like she's having a big moment all on her own. There's so much glory in being her that I can hardly stand myself.

6

LISTEN. THERE ARE BIRDS ON THE ROOF PECKING AT THE gutter . . . a squeaky cart rolling through the grass . . . Chris kicking the woodpile . . . Jericho humming . . . *I know that song. I swear I do.* Chris whispering his lines . . . more humming . . . *What's the name of that song?*

I press my forehead against the tree trunk and shut my eyes, as if I'm counting for hide and seek, but in my mind I'm forcing Rodney into a far corner and Norah into another, hoping they'll stay put.

"Are you okay up there?" Chris asks from the ground beneath me.

"Shhh!" I shoo him with my hand.

Feel. I'm Norah now. I'm Norah. I'm with my brother and his friend and we're going to build a crow's nest. It's going to be our escape from the world.

"I asked her to concentrate," Terrance says. "Give her a minute."

React. Forget the scripts: the blue, the pink, the yellow, the green. Toss them all away. Let them fly.

"Here we go. Let's roll sound," Terrance calls. "And we're rolling, rolling!"

Ready or not, here I come.

I lift my head.

"Action!"

Up in my perch, I sway my foot back and forth and look through the bright leaves at the cloudless sky. Only a few inches below my red Converse, Chris is drilling the fifth wooden rung onto the tree trunk.

"I can't believe you're gonna have your own crow's nest! Why didn't we think of this before?" Jericho raises his voice over the electric drill. "This is genius." I watch him carefully as he measures one piece of wood against another. Then he picks up the saw and cuts the new rung to size.

"All we'll have to do is climb up here every morning, and we'll be able to see right away how the waves are." Chris steps back to check his work. I watch him, and I *listen*. I listen with everything I've got. "No more trekking our boards all the way down to the beach at six in the morning when the water's flat," he says.

Jericho pushes the saw with jerky, uneven strokes. "I'm gonna be over here every day!" Sawdust falls onto his left sneaker.

I roll my eyes. "You're already over here every day," I say. Then I test the newest rung with the tip of my toe. "We'll never have to walk down to the shore again," I say, looking down at the top of Chris's sweaty head. "Except when we want to."

Chris lifts the ladder from against the tree and leans it against the old speedboat that's rotting along the side of the house. It's the spot where Terrance told me to focus, and where I knew Norah hated me.

"Hey, Buzz, maybe three more rungs," Chris says. "That should do it."

"No. Do more!" I tell him. "The higher we get the better!"

Chris wipes his brow. "Four more."

I smile.

"You got it." Jericho wipes his brow.

I know I'm supposed to *feel* like Norah, but I'm thinking *about* her, not *as* her. I'm wondering which of my movies she's seen and who she'd rather have playing her instead of me.

Standing and grasping the tree for balance, I crane my neck to peer through the branches. "Hey, we can even see up the road from up here!"

"A perfect lookout." Chris nods.

"Genius," Jericho says again.

"All's we need now is a pair of binoculars," I say. "Then we can see clear through to the lighthouse. Don't you think?"

"We just might." Chris lifts the drill and revs it up twice like a motorcycle before pushing a screw through the next rung. "I think I can scrounge us up a pair, somewhere."

React. That's what matters most. Just keep reacting and make it look like I'm feeling. I lift my hands and look through a pair of imaginary binoculars. "Or how about one of those old-timey pirate telescopes that stretch! You know the kind I mean?" I adjust my hands and pretend to pull one long scope. "If we get one of those, we'll have it made. We'll be the luckiest kids in Montauk."

"TJ!" Rodney yells from inside the house. We all jump at the sound of his voice. "You dumbass, no-good . . ." He bursts out from the screen door, huffing and puffing. "You put that ladder against my boat!" The spit on his lips stretches and snaps. He grabs the ladder, and I pull my legs up just in time before he slams it against the tree.

"I didn't scratch it or anything!" Chris takes two steps back. "I leaned it, that's all."

My heart is racing, remembering Rodney's weight pressing against my chair.

Rodney holds the metal ladder in front of Chris and shakes it at him. "You piece of shit! How *stupid* can you be?"

I grasp my shoulders where Rodney touched me. I know how he smells and how dry and heavy his hands are.

"Rodney, the boat's not even painted yet!" Jericho says.

"Shut up!" he screams at Jericho. Then he turns all his anger back to Chris. "I've been workin' on that boat for a year!"

Chris sticks his chin out. "From the couch?"

Rodney flings the ladder across the backyard. It crashes and clangs onto the grass. "What did you say, you little turd?" he hisses.

I shrink against the tree.

"You heard me." Chris stands tall; his chest rises and falls. I want him to back down, to run.

Rodney lunges forward, just as Chris dodges away. But Rodney grabs him by the back of his jeans. He lifts Chris off his feet and slams him against the boat.

"TJ!" I scream, and shake.

"Cut!" Terrance calls.

Terrance rubs his eyes and then clears his throat. "We'll do it again. This time, just a beat faster between Chris and Rodney." He holds his fingers up to measure a pinch. "Just a tad." He looks at me and nods.

When he lets out a breath, so do I.

. . . . .

Back in tutoring, I'm supposed to be studying a history chapter on Egyptians. Damon is helping me preread the section questions and showing me how to find bold words in the chapter because those are usually the answers. But I can't concentrate, not when my nerves are still worked up about Rodney and the fight scene keeps churning outside our window. The crew turned the camera around; it's replaced me in the tree so it can film the fight from Norah's point of view. Terrance won't need me again for a long while. I wonder how Chris is doing.

"I'm afraid we're not being very productive," Damon

whispers as we listen to Rodney yelling at Chris. "How about we take a break the next time Terrance calls cut?"

This is fine with me because I'm pretty sure "break" is code for "watch the fight scene." Damon's been sneaking peeks out the window almost as often as I have.

As soon as we get outside, I pick a snack from the craft service table—a package of shortbread cookies—then I sit in a chair behind Terrance and Peter Bustamante where they're watching the monitors.

"Snack break?" Peter asks me.

"Yes."

I want to ask Terrance how I was up in the tree, but the back of his head tells me he isn't in a talking mood. I didn't count how many takes we did, but do know I only messed up three times, maybe three and a half. That's no more or less than the boys, so I think I did pretty okay, even though I felt more like myself than like Norah.

I always feel very professional when I sit in these tall director's chairs. During my first movie, my chair even said TALLU-LAH LEIGH on the back. *The Locals* didn't bother personalizing chairs. That's how I can tell if a movie has a big budget or a small budget. This chair only says CAST, but I still like sitting in it.

Chris is inside the house while the camera is resetting. He's probably working himself up to be upset, or maybe he already is. I wonder if he's been using a trigger.

"Here we go. Let's everyone get back into place. Back to one," Terrance says, and that's when Chris comes out with a hand over his face.

Jericho takes his mark in the middle of the grass, and Chris stands against the boat in front of Rodney, exactly where they stood when I was up in the tree.

"Rolling, rolling!" Terrance calls.

Rodney presses his hand right under Chris's throat and shoves him up against the boat. Just as Chris starts to struggle, Terrance calls, "And . . . action!"

"Get off him!" Jericho jumps on Rodney's back, but Rodney hurls him right off, elbowing Jericho in the temple.

"Listen to me, worthless beach rat." Rodney holds his arm against Chris's chest.

I cover my eyes but peer through my fingers.

"Mouth off to me again and I'll send you and your sister away on a long, long journey, and your mama's never gonna miss you. Hear me?" Rodney plants his big hand on the side of Chris's head as if he's gripping a football. Then he shoves Chris into the dirt. "Good-for-nothing runt."

Chris spits and spurts on his hands and knees.

Terrance has turned his head. Now I can see the side of his face. He's as still as can be, and the color's gone from his skin.

Rodney plants one foot on the ground, the other against the tree, and starts ripping a rung off the trunk. He curses, struggling with the wooden plank, rocking it back and forth until it cracks and the screws rip from the tree. The bark tears away, leaving a splintered, naked wound.

Terrance hasn't checked the lighting or even looked at the screen. He's just staring. I knew it would be a tough day to *play* TJ. But now I realize that it's also a tough day to *be* him.

On the monitor, I watch Chris sitting in the dirt with his knees up. He grips the back of his head with both hands and starts shaking, from his stomach to his chest to his shoulders. He looks up. The camera zooms in close. His face is a mess of dirty tears.

7

VIVA SKIPPED OUT ON OUR LOBSTER DINNER—OR MAYBE she's having it, just not with me. I thought for sure we'd go since Terrance didn't have a bad thing to say about scene 15, but it didn't happen. "We don't have to go now. We can go any night," is what my mother said. I'm not holding my breath. Most times when she talks about doing something it's just daydreaming; the planning is usually the best part.

All week the crew has been barbecuing at the public beach across from the hotel, so I'm walking over to see if Chris is there. My head is swimming with things to tell him after scene 15, like how he was so good I almost cried, even when I wasn't on camera, and about Norah being disappointed with me.

I can't find Chris anywhere at the bonfire. Jericho is here, but he's with his dad. They don't need my company; it looks like they're having a good time taking selfies in front of the fire. That's what it's like on a first movie—everything's exciting, and maybe you'll never get to act again, so you take a picture of the craft service table because you've never seen so many snacks before in your life. And you take pictures of each other in front of the fuzzy boom microphone or a wardrobe rack. Me and Viva used to go nuts with that stuff, too.

One picture we still do on every job is of me in front of my trailer. I stand beside my character's name that's taped to the door: first Tallulah Leigh and then Yoli and then Margaret and now Norah. Some moms measure their kids and mark their height inside a closet. I think of each dressing trailer as the way Viva measures me.

Someday we'll print the pictures out. In houses on TV there's usually family photos framed on a staircase wall. Once we get stairs I'd like to do something like that. But for now our pictures live inside the computer.

Jericho's dad has a real camera (not just a phone). He wears it around his neck like the paparazzi. Jericho said that they're going to make a slideshow for his mother and his little sisters who are home in Chicago. I bet their whole family will eat popcorn and watch the slideshow together on their big-screen TV and talk about what a fun hobby acting is. And isn't it a bonus that now they have some extra fun money for vacation? Lucky them.

I really miss my movie dad, Brian, from *Hit the Road* . . . my Pops. We took lots of pictures together with his scratchy beard against my cheek. Viva says it's good to miss someone; it means that you cared and so did they. But you gotta move on in life. "Say goodbye quick like a bandit," is her advice. I cried for a week when I wrapped *Hit the Road* but for only a few days after *Buy One, Get One* and just a couple hours after *Zany Aces*. Letting go of stuff is a skill to work on like any other.

The beach is divided with movie folks around the bonfire and a new gang of local kids along the shore. I stare at the real locals: the girly types are in short skirts and fluttery bikini tops, strolling in a clump with their arms linked, watching the sporty boys toss a spiraled Nerf football that whistles in the air. It looks like sports sacks are popular here—those drawstring bags you can wear on your back. Some have initials on them; that probably costs extra.

The Montauk girls are giggling up a fuss. I follow their eyes and see Chris scrounging around for something in the tall reeds.

"*Go*, Arianne. *Go!*"

"Omigod, omigod, omigod!"

The local girls push their friend forward—the one in the group with boobs, not little boobs pushed up high, but real-sized ones that jiggle on their own.

The boys stop tossing the ball to nudge each other and laugh at Chris. "Hey, check it out. It's the Crapper!"

In his movie *Camp Magaskawee*, Chris had diarrhea against a tree. The Montauk boys are ripping on him about it, but the girls sure aren't turned off. Arianne fans her face with her hands. Then she does a stupid sashay up to *my* movie brother.

These girls probably think they know Chris, all because they've seen him in *Sixth Period Lunch*. How shocked would they be if they found out that Chris is nothing like that role? He's quiet and shy, not cocky. And he hasn't got moves or pickup lines. He's got worries and wonderings. Suddenly I want to talk to Chris about Rodney, even if I'm not positive Rodney is a full-blown creeper.

But Chris is being polite to Arianne; he's letting her babble on and on, while the whole time he's kicking up sand and looking past her shoulder. She keeps flapping her hands, probably to make up for Chris saying nothing. If I have to tell the truth, she is sort of pretty. But Chris is an actor, so he's used to movie-star pretty. To him Arianne might only be average.

"Hey! This is you, right? Joss Byrd?" one of the local boys asks. He holds his phone to show me a picture of me wearing my specially made multicolored designer Betsey Johnson dress.

"Uh-huh."

"That's so cool. That was at the Oscars, right?" He keeps asking questions about the red carpet, but in my head his voice shrinks into the background because I'm busy watching Chris, who's walking off with Arianne. They're close now, so close that his arm rubs against hers each time he lifts his right foot off the sand. ". . . Did you get to meet Robert Downey, Jr.? How about Mark Wahlberg? He's, like, my favorite actor. Who's yours? Ever see *The Fighter*? It's wicked good."

Some of the guys from our crew are waving Chris over to the bonfire. "Christopher Tate, you dirty dawg!" A greasy-haired guy called Slim, who works the sound for us, pulls Chris over to the side. "Look at her. You should. You *have* to." Slim is pointing at Arianne. Then he whispers to Chris in secret, elbowing him like he's giving sex advice, while Chris shrugs and smiles at the ground. Right about now, I hate Slim. "She's practically begging for it." He raises his voice again. "That's an easy in. You want to, don't you? Well, don't you?"

And Arianne—while the crew is chanting, "Stud! Stud! Stud!"—is mouthing to her girlfriends for them to take her picture with Chris when they walk by. What a sneak. She isn't the girl for Christopher Tate. Arianne's friends are getting their phones ready, holding them real low, as if no one can tell exactly what they're doing.

The sound guy runs back to the bonfire and grabs a six-pack of beer; I hate him so much. I look around for a real grown-up, a responsible one who might care. But that's not as easy to come by as the beer. I'm not sure what Damon does after we wrap on set every night, but he's never come to the bonfire. Chris's own guardian, his Grandma Lorna, reads large-print books and naps all day in the trailer and then goes to bed at eight.

"Slim! Not a good idea," says our wardrobe girl, Monique. Maybe there's hope. "Leave the beer here."

I knew I liked Monique from the start. When we first met her, she was nice enough to listen to my mother ramble about her business idea for dancewear that doubles as shapewear.

"The kid asked me for it!" Slim says, pointing at Chris. "Are

78

you about to say no to number one on the call sheet?" On a film shoot, each actor has a number on the call sheet. I'm two. Number one plays the most important character in the movie.

"Yes, I am, when number one on the call sheet is fourteen years old and his parents are a thousand miles away," Monique says, grabbing at the beer.

"Well, I'm not." Slim pulls the six-pack away and hustles it up to Chris.

"This one is on you, Slim! Don't come crying to me if something happens to that kid!" Monique calls.

And that's that.

Chris holds the beer against his chest as he thanks Slim—it looks like he really did ask for the beer. Now I hate Chris, too, I really do. Obviously he doesn't have Doris Cole for an agent. If he did, he'd know that the other thing that can ruin a child actor besides puberty is a trip to rehab.

Chris is carrying the beer down at his side. Then right in public, in front of people we work with, people who load film into our cameras and hand us our paychecks, he lifts his other arm and drapes it over Arianne's shoulders! How could he? How could he even be so hypnotized by boobs when I really need to ask him: *If I tell you something private about Rodney, will you keep it a secret?*

"That's our boy!" someone yells from the bonfire as if we're all watching Chris in Little League, up at bat.

The Montauk boy is still talking to me. "How'd you start

being an actress?" he wants to know. "Is it the funnest thing ever? Because it looks like it is—auditions and fans and the E! channel? Joss?"

I'm thinking about Rodney and his chest hair poking through his holey undershirt. But the Montauk boy wants a shined-up interview answer about awards shows and limos. He doesn't want the honest truth about all the unscripted parts of my life.

"It's the funnest," I say, finally looking at him.

"Cool." He smiles. "Does this movie need any extras? Like, to walk by on the beach or to sit in a restaurant? I can skateboard."

"Uh, I don't really know."

Chris and Arianne disappear past the sea grass. My neck isn't long enough to follow them any farther. There goes all the stuff I need to say. And for the first time, I don't want to play a child forever; I want to grow up already and be a hot girl.

"Hey, can I ask your professional opinion? What do you think of acting classes? I mean, are they a good idea or . . . because there's a workshop here on the weekends. But if you think it's lame . . ."

"I don't take classes," I say.

"No. I didn't think so. I mean, of course not. Okay. So, wait. No workshop?"

"Well, if you want." What does he care what I think? If he can read then he's already miles ahead of me. And if he wants

80

to take a workshop, then he should take a workshop. If he doesn't, then he shouldn't. Who am I to stop him from becoming his favorite flower?

"Ray! Hey, blowtard!" When I turn around, I see the surfer girl from the parking lot with her shorts low and her attitude high. "Keri's lookin' for you—Keri, your *girlfriend*," she says, adjusting her dozen bracelets. One of her thick leather straps is branded: GWEN.

"Do you know who this is? I'm talking to *Joss Byrd*, from *Buy One, Get One*," Ray says, as if I'm not standing right next to him. "She's worked with the coolest actors and she's not owned by Disney, which is, like, career suicide."

"So?" Gwen shrugs.

"Whaddaya mean, so? *Buy One, Get One* was nominated for Best Picture!" He lifts his phone, showing her my photo. "At the Academy Awards! Dang it, Gwen, you know I've always wanted to be an actor."

She smirks. "Since when?"

"Since always. *High School Musical*."

"Pfft."

Gwen is so cool she doesn't even care about being cool. If she did, she'd probably comb her hair or redo her nails before they chipped down to dirty bits of black polish. Gwen would crush the kids back in Tyrone, Pennsylvania, who only think they're cool. I'd love to have a head-to-toe makeover to look like Gwen. I bet if I went back to Tyrone looking just like her, they'd never stuff my backpack with sweat socks again. What would be best would be if I had the makeover and then switched schools. My new classmates wouldn't know me any other way. I would start cool. A cool actor.

"Nice meeting you, Joss," Ray says.

"You too," I answer, even though he never actually introduced himself.

"Can I get a picture?" he asks. Before I even answer, he holds up his phone, scooches beside me, and snaps away. I wish I'd had my makeover already. "Thanks." He checks the picture before running off. I probably look goofy in it. He didn't even let me see.

Gwen looks me up and down. She's judging me without even trying to hide it. "I've never heard of you."

"Well, I haven't really done movies that kids watch, just dramas and stuff."

"Huh." She flips her hair over her shoulder.

. . . . .

"Where's your project?" Bella Pratt thinks she's so great because she always brings her homework on time and always remembers which days to bring an art smock and which days to bring gym clothes. I can't keep those days straight; I'm not around often enough to get them right.

"I dunno." We had a project due?

"You didn't make your electrical circuit?" Bella shoves her

82

wooden board toward me, showing off cardboard buildings with lightbulbs and wires and switches: Bella Pratt's City of Lights!

"I missed the unit because I was on set. I had books but not bulbs and stuff." I don't mention that I forgot my books at the studio and production will have to mail them to me overnight. In my backpack is just lunch and my sweatshirt.

"What do you mean, you were on set?"

"A movie set. It's a movie called Zany Aces. I filmed it in Los Angeles."

"You're full of it," Bella says, as if I could or would lie about being in a movie.

"Why would I lie? You can just look it up." If she's so smart, she should know how to use the Internet.

"I've never seen you in anything," she says while her friends gather around with their lightbulbs on trays, in boxes, or glued to poster board. "None of us have."

"Just because you don't know something doesn't mean it isn't true," I say. I should steal one of her wires so that the bulbs won't light up when she presents her project. I think I will.

"Yeah?" Bella puffs up her chest to play tough in front of her friends. "Well, maybe if you didn't miss so much school for nothing you wouldn't be so stupid," she says.

• • • • •

"Ray's my best friend's boyfriend, you know," Gwen says as Ray catches up to a girl with long, dark braids and hugs her. He sinks his hands into the girl's back pockets. Braids look so childish on me. I could never pull them off; I'd look like I'm five. But on that girl they're stylish. The fashion channels would call her "hippie chic." Ray and Keri remind me of stuffed monkeys Velcroed together. "They've been going out three months," Gwen says. I'm impressed, I guess; three months is the whole summer, plus part of an entirely different school year. "So, what, you think that just because you're making a movie you can come to Montauk and take over our beach and talk to our guys?"

Me? That guy wasn't talking to *me*. He was talking to *Joss Byrd: friend of Robert Downey, Jr.*

"What's the matter?" Gwen leans back as if she's making room to put up her dukes. "You don't know what to say without a script?"

I don't know what to say *with* a script. "I'm just here for work," I say, trying to keep my voice steady. "It's . . . my job."

"It's your job to hog our waves and to hang out on the beach with an older girl's boyfriend?"

"He was just asking if he could be an extra."

"An extra? Ha!" Gwen scratches her head and mumbles under her breath, "*High School Musical.*" I can see the bonfire reflecting in her eyes—two flames roaring back at me. Gwen lifts her phone, which is vibrating and lighting up in her palm. "Arianne and Chris Tate are hooking up in shed," she reads. She taps to open the photo and scrunches her face. "Gross." She

84

swipes the picture away. "She didn't waste any time. But I'm sure your friend will be very happy with her services. She is Montauk Point's employee of the month, every month."

"What do you mean?" I ask.

"I mean she does a lot of *jobs*. You know—hand and blow?" Gwen says, motioning each job with her fist. "Arianne is foul. We're in *eighth* grade. What's she gonna do when we get to high school?"

I can't imagine what Chris is doing or what Arianne is doing to him in that picture. I don't ever want to see it. I'm dying to see it.

" 'Check out how hot I am! I messed around with an actor in the shed next to a bucket of live worms.' I'll have to listen to that romantic tale for the rest of my life, now." Gwen rolls her eyes and sends a text back. "See? This is exactly what I mean . . ." She glares at me again, fires raging, as if this is my fault, as if I wanted this to happen.

The phone lights up again in her hand. Every flash makes me imagine something worse—Chris kissing Arianne, her shirt up, her hand down his shorts—I can't stop picturing stuff. This isn't the Golden Age of Hollywood. It's modern times. I know that clothing is optional and the action doesn't fade after kissing.

"It's always the same. You movie people take our bonfire and our waves and turn our town into Whoretauk Point." Gwen stuffs her phone into her back pocket as she walks away. "Some very good *work* you're doing," she grumbles. "Keep it up, every-one!" she calls to the crew with her thumbs up.

For no reason, I walk over to the food and fill a plate. I don't want anything. I lost my appetite one whoretauk ago. My stomach hurts just looking at the barbecue chicken. The glaze is too orange, and I'm not sure it's cooked all the way through; it's too dark out to tell. But there's nothing else to do but eat while I'm waiting for Chris to finish his not-so-secret rendez-vous, so I take my barbecue chicken to a quiet spot and make the best of things.

I thought that my stomach couldn't get queasier, but I was wrong because Rodney is heading in my direction with a plate and a drink. Why's he coming over here? There are plenty of other people he can talk to—people who aren't twelve-year-old girls.

Don't look at him. That way he won't feel invited. *Can't sit here!* I pick up a reed and play with it, as if it's the most fasci-nating reed that's ever sprouted. I should've stayed with the crowd. How many times have I heard about safety in numbers? That's another one of my problems. I don't think of important things until it's too late.

Finally, Chris is on his way back. This isn't the time for me to dwell on Arianne when Rodney's on the prowl. *Hurry, Chris, hurry!* Chris has his hands in his pockets; he's just strolling along, as if my safety isn't at stake over here. The closer he gets, the clearer I see his guilty, doofy expression.

Jericho runs at him, and then he laughs and jumps on Chris and rubs his head. All that's missing is a cooler of Gatorade.

Rodney has stopped to watch, too, as Slim rushes over to meet the boys.

"Really? Yeah? Yeah?" Slim yells. He slaps Chris on the back and shakes his hand. Chris lowers his bright red face.

When Rodney sees Chris walking my way, he turns toward the trail back to the Beachcomber. That was close. I must've been tensed up this whole time because now all my muscles are relaxing. I could roll over and fall asleep here and now.

"Hey," Chris says.

Why am I embarrassed? I haven't done anything, but I feel embarrassed anyway. I don't look up, can barely look at him. But really, all I want to do is look—at his face, his hands, his body. Did he get a job? Or something more?

"What's up?" he asks, all innocently. He really is a talented actor.

"Nothin'."

Chris takes a seat beside me on a hollow log.

Maybe he's messed around with a lot of girls, and this is just a day in the life of Christopher Tate. If that's the case, why would he care about what I have to say about Rodney or Norah or anything else? I trace circles in the sand with the reed until it breaks. Then I throw the pieces into the dunes.

"Why are you being weird?" Chris asks.

Because it is weird. Because you just did stuff with a whoretauk, stuff I can't even talk about, and right now I need you to be my movie brother. "I'm not being weird."

He laughs as he watches Jericho gabbing away with the crew. "Jericho's nuts. He doesn't know what he's talking about half the time."

"Yeah."

"You think he'll keep acting after this?"

"Probably." Nobody ever leaves unless they're forced to leave—puberty or rehab.

"Don't tell him I told you this, okay?" Chris says.

"What?" I look up at him without blinking. Maybe he didn't do anything with Arianne after all. Maybe she wasn't his type or maybe she said something idiotic or had bad breath.

He leans his shoulder softly against mine. "I used the drops."

"You *did*?" I stare, surprised that he used them and even more surprised that he's telling me.

"I tried not to, but I couldn't make it happen." He shakes his head.

"Wow," I say. "It was the best scene so far, though. I think Terrance wanted to cry. I know I almost did." The drops don't change a thing, if you ask me. Tears you can fake, but you can't fake pain.

"Long day." Chris sighs. "Anyway, I'm glad it's over."

He doesn't even know about Norah or Rodney. "Same here."

"Hey, I found you something." Chris digs into his pocket and hands me a piece of purple sea glass, an almost-perfect triangle that fits right between my thumb and pointer finger. It's warm from his body heat. "Thought you'd like it."

I hold it up to my eye; it glows against the fire. "I do." How long does it take for all the sharp edges to wear down until it's this smooth? Months? Years? "It's like a guitar pick," I say. Sometimes I hear Chris strumming a guitar in his trailer. I wish I could play. Brian, my Pops, wanted to teach me during *Hit the Road*, but we never had time. "Where'd you find it?"

"Right along the grass there." He points to the spot where I watched him disappear.

"Just now?" I can't help but ask. I don't want the sea glass to be tainted by Arianne. It'd be gross if it was in Chris's pocket when he fooled around with her.

"Uh, just . . . before."

"Oh." Heat rushes to my cheeks as I try not to imagine him and her doing who-knows-what.

I rub the sea glass into my palm till it feels like it's about to melt into my skin. I guess it shouldn't matter when he found it. The point is, he cares about me. *I found you something . . . I found you something . . .* And he could've given the sea glass to Arianne, but he didn't. He gave it to me, his movie sister.

"Hey, Chris?"

"Yeah?"

"Don't tell Jericho, okay?"

He scrunches his eyebrows. "What?"

"I met the real Norah, and she hates me." I frown. "She thinks I'm the worst actress ever."

Chris sucks in his breath.

"And . . . there's something else. It's bad."

Doris would say it's unpleasing to talk about a costar. But the way Chris is looking at me makes me sort of proud to have something major to tell him. "It's about Rodney. He might be a perv for real."

"What? Why?" He looks at me with wild eyes. "What'd he do?"

"He came into my schoolroom and skeeved me out. He went like this." I grab my shoulders and cringe. "I wasn't sure it was anything. But just now he was trying to come over here, except you came."

Chris's mouth drops open. "Oh, shit."

Telling Chris makes Rodney more real. But I'm not afraid. I'm relieved. Across the beach everyone else is still eating and drinking and talking nonsense, which is so strange when we've got serious stuff going on here. There's even a song playing, "Lifting me up, baby, higher and higher . . ." I'm glad there's music, though. This way no one can hear us.

"And Chris?" If I confess one last thing, maybe I'll feel relieved about it, too. "Remember that day when I kicked you guys out of my schoolroom?"

"Yeah," he says. The bonfire is blazing in his eyes.

Viva would say it's a mistake to tell him. It's too big a risk. But I lean closer now because it's also too big a secret to hide any longer. "Well, the truth is . . ." I rub my thumb against my sea glass for a moment. "I'm not a 'big deal,'" I whisper. "I'm not *Joss Byrd*. I'm an unofficial dyslexic."

8

SO WHAT IF I'M NOT THE ONLY GIRL WHO SHARED TONIGHT with Christopher Tate? I might not be hot stuff like Arianne. But for now, I'm deciding that it's more special to swap secrets than to swap spit. I didn't even feel so left out when he went off to eat corn on the cob with Jericho. They can have their boy-talk because my time with Chris can be measured better by bonding than by minutes.

Chris said there's different types of intelligences, like logical intelligence and visual intelligence. He saw a video about it in school. He explained that since I'm a natural actress, I've got extra interpersonal intelligence. If we added up my total smartness, I might possibly be more intelligent than most people.

He also told me I couldn't argue about it because it's not based on his opinion. It's science. So I have to believe him.

After all that today has thrown my way, I'm going to sleep like a rock; it's felt like ten days in one. At least I have thoughts of Chris to think about now—that beats falling asleep to thoughts of Norah or Rodney. Sliding my key card in the door is nearly as good as laying my head on my pillow.

But something's different about our room.

The sliding door is wide open.

The TV is blaring.

I recheck the room number.

204.

The sheets are moving.

My mother is giggling.

There's a man's voice.

And then his arm.

And shoulder.

He's moving on top of her, moaning my mother's name.

Her leg is hooked over his body.

He lifts his chest.

And his head.

It's not just any man.

It's *Terrance*.

I'm hyperventilating again. My room card slips from my fingers right before I step back outside. As soon as the door clicks, I turn and punch the wooden railing. Then I press my forehead against it.

How could she do this?

He's my director!

We're supposed to listen to him about when to scream and

when to be still. We're supposed to start when he says action and stop when he says cut. And that's *it*.

Nobody—especially not my mother—is supposed to bring him to their hotel room to do it with him while the rest of the town is eating chicken!

And everybody who's ever seen a *People* magazine knows that he's *married*!

There are so many rules that I have to follow: get to set on time, hang my wardrobe at the end of the night, know all the crew members' names, say please and thank you, keep my trailer clean, don't talk bad about other actors, hand out wrap-gifts to the cast and crew, don't let anyone find out that I'm stupid, don't complain, don't complain, don't complain . . .

What are the rules for my mother?

. . . . .

"It's the director!" Viva loud-whispers with one hand over the phone. On her laptop are dozens of pictures of Terrance Rivenbach—him in a baseball cap, him in a tuxedo, him standing on a cliff, him playing basketball with the president (of the country!) . . . "Well, if you say so. I mean, if you truly think my daughter is right for the part . . . Right . . . I can understand that . . . You did? . . . Yes, we have worked with them before . . . Of course . . ." I recognize something in Viva's voice. They're "clicking," as she likes to put it. With some people she just "clicks," and there you go.

"But still. I'd hate to fly her across the country if she isn't

exactly right," Viva says, even though she would never turn down a paid trip to LA for any reason whatsoever. "I don't like pulling her out of school."

I'm laughing to myself, already planning to charge my laptop before the flight so it'll last through a couple movies.

"Well, if you really think so . . ." Viva scrolls through the pictures on the screen and clicks on one of the director with his pretty young wife and their very blond twin boys. "I very much look forward to meeting you, too."

. . . . .

I should've known this would happen. She's going to ruin everything the way she always does. Any minute now she'll piss Terrance off; he'll hate her, and then he'll hate me, too.

I wonder if Peter Bustamante knows. Is this the image she wants to give to the executive producer? And if Doris finds out she'll be furious. How does my mother expect us to look professional when she's pulling stuff like this? People will think we're a joke.

I plop down against the door and breathe into my knees—deep breath in, deep breath out. All I can think about is one of my triggers: we lost the house we loved in Maryland because Viva wanted to follow her beefed-up boyfriend to Tyrone, Pennsylvania.

"It's gonna be so great!" she said. "Brendan and I are partnering with his friends and opening up a chain of upscale hair salons. There aren't any classy places yet. The whole town is hungry for something high-end. We'll buy the land and his friends will build. We'll grow our money back faster than we can count it."

But Tyrone wasn't great. It was a broken-down apartment with stained carpets and jittery lightbulbs and other people's scum between the tiles. Viva was only right about one thing— there isn't anything classy in the entire town. Tyrone is a place to leave, not to go. The town's hungry, all right. There's not even a Panera Bread. Sophisticated salons didn't make sense from day one. Why would people who wear pajama pants to Walmart pay sixty dollars for a haircut?

. . . . .

"When are they building, Brendan? When?" My mother is scream-ing in our kitchen.

"The banks backed out," Brendan says, pacing back and forth.

"They backed out? You said this was a done deal, a sure thing! I already bought the land! And for what? For nothing?" My mother's voice rises higher and higher as she takes Brendan's favorite CD out of the player and grabs a few others off the counter. "We're gonna have to start all over again. Two movies! It took us two movies to make that money!"

What does she mean by "us"? I made those movies. I'm the one who has to start all over again.

96

She takes the CDs and stuffs them in the blender.

"Take your hands off that blender!" Brendan rushes toward her.

"Don't come any closer!" She hops onto my step stool with the blender over her head, like she's a crazy Statue of Liberty.

Brendan holds a hand up to calm her. "Those are live Pearl Jam recordings. I can't buy those CDs again! You press that button, Viva, and you'll be sorry."

Viva presses the button. "I'm already sorry! I'm sorry I ever met you!" she yells, as the blender sputters and crunches.

"You bitch!" Brendan picks up the whole CD player and smashes it against the wall. His fat, stinking bulldog, Doughboy, is howling into the air.

"What's that? I can't hear you!" My mother holds the blender in her arms. "I'm playing some CDs!" she yells over the racket.

I'm pressed against the wall, covering my ears, remembering our little white house in Maryland; there were snails stuck to the pier, and our neighbors had a yellow boat with a bell on the top. They used to let me pull their crab traps out from the bottom of the water. When we pulled them out of the cage, the crabs, with their speckled blue shells and their googly eyes, would snap their claws and link together like paper dolls.

"You're out of your mind!" Brendan crouches to put Doughboy on his leash. "I'm out of here."

"Good! Go!" Viva steps down to the floor. "We were better off without you!"

The CDs rattle and grind faster and faster. Brendan is throwing his laundry into a garbage bag. I stare at the blender and watch the CDs turn to dust. Dust!

Viva yanks the cord from the wall. The blender stops. She watches Brendan start the car and drive out of our lives. Now we really have nothing here in Tyrone—not even music.

· · · · ·

I stretch my legs across the sandy wooden planks. There are dead insects above me trapped inside the light cover. For some reason, live bugs are fighting to get in. Take it from me: sometimes we're better off in the dark.

I could try to walk to basecamp and sleep in my dressing trailer, if it's open. The sofa flattens into a bed. I could pee there, too; even have a shower if I really want to. Does it need the motor on for the water to pump? But there aren't any towels. I wonder if there are enough paper towels to dry my whole body. Wouldn't the kids at school love that—me living in a trailer, where they think I belong? My head finds the corner between the door and wall. Maybe if I close my eyes, Terrance will leave any minute. My mother says you can't help who you're attracted to. She calls it passion, but I call it a pain in the A-S-S. That I can spell. And according to her, there are two kinds of married men. She's never said what the two kinds are, but thanks to Terrance naked in my mother's bed, I'm learning by example.

. . . . .

"Joss? Joss?" Chris is shaking me awake.

"Huh?" I rub my sore neck. "What time is it?"

"It's late. Where's Viva?"

"Inside," I say softly.

"Then what are you doing out here? Is she asleep?"

"No. She's with someone."

"What do you mean? Like, a *guy*?"

I nod. Too embarrassed to look up but too tired to lie, I say, "Like . . . *Terrance*."

"What?" He lowers onto his knee. "What are they doing?"

"God! What do you *think* they're doing? They're *screwing*."

"Holy . . ."

I hang my head while Chris goes through a dozen *really*s and *are you sure*s.

"Well, just come to my room, then," he says.

"No. I'll get in trouble if I'm not back."

"You can't just sit here listening to them." He stands and stares at the door. I don't really hear anything, just commercials. "We'll leave her a note. Let's go, get up," he says, kicking my feet.

In his room a few doors down, Chris scribbles on the Beachcomber notepad. His room is exactly like ours except it smells like Vicks VapoRub and hard-boiled eggs. He steps out, leaving me with his Grandma Lorna who's asleep in her bed with her mouth open. Her dyed orange hair is thin and faded around her face. Except for the triangle folded under her chin and the lump of her body, her bed is still made. I want my own bed in room 204 so bad. My pj's are tucked under my pillow waiting for me, all soft and cool and smelling like sleep.

There's a bunch of scripts on Chris's coffee table—not *The Locals*. New scripts. I wonder if any of them are worth missing more high school for.

Chris closes the door and pushes the latch. "You can take my bed. I'll just sleep on the end there." He points at his snoring grandmother. That's a big sacrifice, I can tell you that.

While Chris washes up in the bathroom I pull off my sneakers and crawl into his bed. I'm so tired I can't stay awake long enough to thank him.

9

SANDY FEET AND STICKY PITS. BARBECUE SAUCE ON MY fingers, in my mouth, on my chin. The smell of firewood in my hair. I wake up feeling gross all over.

"Joss, honey? Are you awake?" Grandma Lorna says. "When is your call time?" Chris's grandma pulls the drapes open to a bright, sunny morning in Montauk Point.

"Ten. I have tutoring and a fitting." My voice crackles. The other bed is empty, and the shower is running.

"It's eight thirty now. Christopher told me your mother didn't come home last night. Do you want to go check for her now? There's a van that goes to basecamp at nine. You should go then so you can have breakfast."

"Okay." I jam my feet into my sneakers without untying the laces. Then, after pulling the latch flat so that the door doesn't lock behind me, I shuffle to my room.

At the foot of 204 is a note with a rock still on top of it:

Joss is in my room.—Chris

My mother and Terrance could still be inside, so I stand here watching the family next door checking out of their room. The mom and the kids are pushing their luggage outside the door while the dad is pulling the plugs on their inflatable tubes and pressing the air out. I bet if I asked really sweetly, they'd take me home with them. We could play I Spy in the car. When we got home they could officially adopt me. I'd be a good older sister. I'd teach stuff like not to wrestle too loudly in a hotel with thin walls. Our next trip to Montauk would be a real vacation. I wouldn't have to work a single day. I'd just float around the pool on an inflatable sea horse.

I wait for their tubes to deflate before leaving the note right where it is and dragging my feet back to Chris's room. I want to lie to Chris's grandma and say that Viva is back and everything's fine. But where will I go then? The crew's already at basecamp; I don't want them to see me looking like yesterday's leftovers.

"She's not back," I say. There's no way around it.

Grandma Lorna shakes her head and tsk-tsk-tsks, which must be the universal language for "what a terrible mother." Chris's own parents are so busy with their restaurant that they don't come to the set at all, so I don't know what makes Grandma Lorna so high and mighty. "Has she done this kind of thing before?" she asks.

What does she mean by "this kind of thing"? Does my mother sleep around? Does she pick guys over me? That's none of this lady's business. I don't like anybody judging my mother no matter what she does or doesn't do. That's my job. Viva has brought dates home before, but never on location. But this is for me to know and nobody else.

Grandma Lorna pulls her sweater tight around her body as if the thought of my mother gives her the chills. "Do you think we should call somebody?"

"No. It's okay," I say, like it's no biggie. I'd rather eat under-cooked barbecue chicken every meal for the rest of my life than show her how upset I am. "She'll be at the trailer by ten."

"Well . . . if you're sure," she says.

My mother might leave me hanging, but she'd never miss a call time. She knows I have a fitting; she's required to super-vise. "I'm sure. She'll be there."

"All right, then. Let's get you ready for the day." She passes her eyes over me as if I'm trash with trash for a mother. "Would you like to take a shower?"

I would, but not here, and not without a change of clothes. "No. Terrance wants my hair dirty. It's got carrot oil in it from hair and make-up." This is true but not true. He does want my hair dirty, and they did put carrot oil in it. But if I want to wash my hair, I'm allowed. My hairstylist would redo it.

"Well, if you say so," says Grandma Lorna, not convinced. "But I think I have an extra toothbrush around somewhere."

I want so bad to say no to anything more she has to offer.

But because of that nasty barbecue, what else can I do but take her charity?

. . . . .

When I get to *The Locals* basecamp, Viva is at the breakfast truck ordering an omelet. She's had a shower and washed her hair. She's downright shiny and rosy-cheeked, which is a lot more than I can say for myself.

"Good mornin', daughter of mine," Viva says, full of sunshine and rainbows. With her arm around my shoulders, she glances at the line of hungry crew behind her. "Can you throw on the usual for Joss?" she calls up to the cook, and runs her hand over my head. "Did you guys have a fun sleepover?"

Sleepover? What does she think? We made popcorn and watched Frozen?

I answer under my breath, "No. Did *you*?"

"Joss, not now." She presses her shampooed head against my greasy scalp. It's a phony hug to show to the crew.

"How could you?" I mumble.

She pulls me roughly out of the line. "Get in the trailer."

"Ow!" I say, wriggling in her grip. "You're acting like Oscar Coombs!"

"Shush!" Viva digs her fingers into me while she smiles at Peter Bustamante, Benji, Jericho, and his father. "Good morning," she says as she shoves me forward across the lot.

"Don't ever say the name Oscar Coombs to me! Get inside." Viva pushes me up the steps of the school trailer.

Damon is sitting at the table with his breakfast and juice, his eyes wide.

The closing door rattles the entire trailer. "How dare you speak to me like that in front of everybody."

"How *could* you?" I ask again, crossing my arms. *He's my director! You got tsked by an old lady three times, and I had to use a plastic-wrapped emergency toothbrush from a Ramada Inn!*

"I don't answer to you, missy. *You* answer to *me*." She points an angry finger. "I don't care who you are when you're on set. There are no movie stars in this family. I'm still the parent, and you're the kid."

Could've fooled me.

I've heard this before. A zillion times before, actually. In *Paper Moon*. Tatum's dad says, "Don't you go makin' the decisions. I make the decisions. All you gotta do is look like a pretty little girl."

"Wipe that look off your face." Viva swipes her hand in front of my eyes. "Know your place."

I shouldn't say anything. I know I shouldn't, but I've got so much building up inside me, I just can't help myself. "Why do I have to be perfect, but you can do whatever you want?" I yell.

I brace myself for I don't know what—a smack, a thunderbolt, a natural disaster? She's yanked me and shaken me before, but she's never slapped me. Yet. At the table, Damon is eating Tater Tots as if they're popcorn, and he's watching me and my mother like we're entertainment.

105

In a second, Viva's laughing like a crazy person; her eyes are about to pop out of her head. "*Perfect?* What makes you think you're perfect?" She laughs even harder and pulls at her hair. "Get over yourself. And you better watch it, because you're getting mouthier and mouthier with every passing day." She looks in the mirror and adjusts herself. "You're not the only one who deserves a little bit of attention from this world."

But I never wanted attention from the world. I only wanted attention from her.

"Don't forget that you're just one zit and a training bra away from being unemployable." She slams the door behind her.

That's one line I can't ever forget.

"Who's Oscar Coombs?" Damon asks. I almost forgot he was here. I should probably be embarrassed, but I'm not because he already knows all our business, and none of it has shocked him so far. Someday he'll be one of those people who's interviewed about my life story. I wonder what he'll decide to keep to himself for "life or longer."

"Cameron Coombs, the kid actor's father. He had a tantrum on set. He broke a camera and got arrested."

"Oh, right. I read about that." Damon scratches his head. "What ever happened to Cameron Coombs? I never see him anymore."

I stare blankly. "Exactly."

"Ah . . ." Damon holds his breakfast burrito and pushes a bowl of pistachios and melon across the table. "Nuts?"

Plunking into a chair, I pick up a pistachio but trade it back for a slice of melon.

"You weren't at the bonfire last night," I say.

"It was a school night," Damon answers, unfolding a napkin.

Of course. Our one responsible adult was in bed by nine.

Through the screen door I see Benji crossing the parking lot with my breakfast. I open the door and crouch down for the handoff.

"Breakfast! Your usual." Benji reaches up to pass me my foil-covered plate of French toast and scrambled eggs. It's warm in my palm, and I smell the sweet maple syrup.

"You all right, Joss?" Benji asks softly.

What is there to say but "A-okay"?

"Good." Benji winks.

Before the audition for Tallulah Leigh, me and Viva day-dreamed a lot about being served drinks beside a swimming pool where there's live music and a buffet table with crab legs. I always pictured a cruise ship or that Sandals resort on the commercial. But now we've got even more, so I'm not about to complain.

"Your fitting will be sometime after lunch. I'll swing by and bring you and Viva over," Benji says. "Can I get you anything else while you start tutoring?" I can tell he's not just asking because it's his job.

"Uh . . . yeah, one thing." I lean over my food to whisper. "Can you ask Monique in wardrobe if she's got something I can wear for now? Nothing special—just a regular top and shorts? Because it's getting hot, and I'm in *these*." I pull on my thick gray sweatpants, which I wore to last night's bonfire.

"Done," he answers, no questions asked.

Some people like to boss around production assistants because they're the fetchers around here. Directors and actors and producers are always telling them: fetch me some coffee, fetch me the paper, fetch me the copies. Worst of all, I've seen actors make them hold an umbrella for them in the rain. I would never do that. I'd feel bad letting someone get wet just so I could stay dry.

"Thank you. You're all the rage, Benji," I say.

He walks away toward the wardrobe truck and calls, "And Joss Byrd, you are the latest craze!"

After I step back inside the trailer, I notice a fat envelope on the counter. I freeze. "What is that?" I ask Damon. It's the kind of envelope with a metal clasp—the kind that usually holds contracts or headshots to autograph . . . or scripts.

Damon opens the clasp. He peeks inside as if what's in there might bite him.

"It's another one, isn't it?"

"Sorry."

"I give up." I lay my head on the table. "What color is it *now*?" I ask, as if it makes any difference.

He pulls the entire script out. The color reminds me of stale Halloween candy.

"Ew. Orange," I say.

"Actually"—Damon reads the cover page—"it's called . . . goldenrod. It's the 'goldenrod revision.'"

"What about the lines?" I ask. "Is the order different or are the words different?"

He flips pages and pauses. "The words are different."

Goldenrod is the most hideous color I've ever seen.

10

"Hiya, cutie," the lady in the very clean, white shirt says. "Can you stand on that piece of tape for me and tell the camera your name and your age and where you're from and a little bit about yourself?"

"Uh-huh." I put my toes behind the pink tape. "Here?"

"That's perfect. Go ahead. Your name, please."

"I'm Joss. Byrd. I'm six."

"And where are you from?"

"Maryland. Our backyard is water."

"How fun," she says. "Now, can you turn and face left for me?"

I turn in one direction. I hope it's left.

"Good. And now turn and face right?"

I turn in the other direction.

"Great. You can face forward," she says. "Did you drive all the way from Maryland to meet us?"

"Uh-huh."

"That's impressive. And how'd you like traveling all those miles?"

"Our air conditioning busted."

I don't know why she's laughing. It was so hot; I could've fainted. Sometimes kids die in cars. I saw it twice on the news.

"Oh, no," she says. "Well, I hope you have a better ride home."

"We're gonna stay in a hotel. An air-conditioned one. With room service."

"Ooh, swanky!" She writes something down on her notepad. That must've been the right answer. "Well, this movie is about a country music singer and his daughter. He's trying to make it big, and she's keeping him company on the road. Do you know anything about country music, Joss?"

"Um . . . I like duets?" I say, like a question even though it's not.

"Oh, nice. Me too. What do you like about them?"

"Me and my mom sing them in the car—like 'Fallin' Away Again'?"

"How sweet." She steps back and lifts a regular camera, not the video kind. "You didn't happen to bring a head shot with you, did you? A picture?"

I want to cry now. "No."

"That's all right. It's not a problem. I'm going to take your picture now, then. Okay?"

"Uh-huh." Before I think to smile she's already done clicking. I won't tell my mother; she'll be mad.

"It was nice meeting you, Joss. Byrd."

. . . . .

111

"Did you know I didn't have to read at my first audition? I didn't even have to smile. I only answered some questions, and that was it," I say. "That's how come I became an actor. After that first job, I just kept getting hired over and over again. It was just luck. That's all. If they'd made me read first off, I never would've been here."

"Did your mother tell you that?" Damon asks.

"She didn't have to. If my first job was, like, *Paper Moon*, with all those lines, I would've completely . . ." I screw up my mouth and give a thumbs-down. "Have you seen *Paper Moon*? It's black and white but on purpose."

"Years ago. I don't remember it much."

"Tatum O'Neal and her dad are con artists." I reach into my book bag and show him the DVD cover. "They pull scams to trick people into giving them money. You should watch it again. Some people don't appreciate it the first time. I know every single word by heart. The best is when she's yelling at him because he owes her money. He keeps saying that he doesn't have it. And she says—"

Damon holds a hand up. "Wait a second. What did you just say?"

"I said the best part is when—"

"No, no. I meant, how did you do that?" Damon asks, very interested. "How did you memorize every single word by heart?"

I rub my thumbs across the DVD picture of Tatum sitting

on a cardboard cutout of a moon. "I just did. I've seen it a zillion times, so—"

"Bull's-eye!" Damon points at me. "I can't believe I'm saying this, but let's forget about reading altogether."

"What?"

He chucks the goldenrod script aside. "For now, I mean, to help you with this scene. We can do your schoolwork a little later, all right?" He opens his computer and starts typing. "This is what we'll do. We'll record the dialogue on my computer so you can listen to it a zillion times. Now, what scene do you have tomorrow?"

"Scene twenty-two," I say, trying to catch up to Damon in my head. "Me and the boys are hungry. But we don't want to go home, so we break into the drive-thru deli."

"Okay. Good. We'll record scene twenty-two. I'll do the boys' lines. Then I'll pause the recording and coach you before your lines. Good idea?"

"Maybe . . ." I try to think of reasons it won't work, but I can't come up with any.

"When we're done recording, you can listen to it over and over until you have it memorized. Then we'll practice Vern LaVeque's listening and reacting, and we'll be golden." Damon smiles. "You'll know your lines inside and out just as well as you know *Paper Moon*. You'll be a wizard! What do you think?"

I actually think I can do this. "Let's try it!" I say, slapping the table. I feel like Helen Keller at the pump. *Water! Water!*

Water! Doris took me to that play in Manhattan last year. Now *that's* a dream role—no lines.

"And if you like this method you can use it for school, too. You can download audio books and record vocabulary definitions or history and science facts that you need to memorize."

I can't think that far ahead. I just want to record my dialogue so that I can start memorizing.

Damon clicks a few keys and swivels the laptop for me to see better. "This is a program called Live Studio. It's supposed to be awesome. I got it to record some keyboard stuff, but I haven't used it yet." The screen shows a control panel with switches and knobs and meters. "I've been composing this one piece for years, and I'm hoping Live Studio might help me to finally finish it." A second tab pops up where Damon adjusts black and gray buttons. "I've written a couple of songs for my friends' band. But this one I'm stuck on is different, more jazzy."

"Okay, okay, Live Studio," I say. "Whatever. Let's start!"

"Just a second, Speedy McSpeederson. I'm still setting it up." He types and clicks. "I haven't initialized the program yet." He looks at me. "And why is it that when I tell you one thing about me, all you can say is 'Hurry up already, Damon. Whatever, Damon'?" He holds up a palm that means "talk to the hand." "Meanwhile, I know that you live in Pennsylvania. I know your favorite movie. I know that you eat French toast and eggs with syrup on the side every morning. I even know that you wear

a"—he points to a shoe box from my wardrobe sneakers—
"size four."

"Sorry." I bite my lip. "I'm just excited to do this."

"That's okay. I'm glad you're excited. But even so. It's a big
world, Joss. And this whole movie business is not all there is.
It's good to learn about other people."

"Hey, I know about people. I know enough about them to pretend to be them. And I know plenty about the rest of the world,"
I argue. "Why do you think I try so hard to be in this one?"

"You're right. I apologize." He nods. "You have seen a lot.
But I still think you should learn about others on a personal level
rather than just an observational level."

I'm rolling my eyes, but I guess it's true that I hardly know
anything about Damon. I didn't even think he wanted me to
know about him. "Okay," I say. "I'll ask about you, then."

"Go ahead," he says as he clicks some more keys. "What
would you like to know? Ask me anything."

I think for a second. "Do you want to be a musician more
than a teacher, like be in the band with your friends?"

"Yes. And no. I wanted to study music in college, but my
father wouldn't let me. He wanted to make sure that I'd always have a stable job, so I had to pick something more practical. Your mother and my father would get along great," he
laughs.

I stare at Damon's hair as he talks. The spikes make good
sense now. He does look like a musician. And he's really pale,

even here at the beach; he's almost see-through. Paleness is very musician-like. I think he has a hole in his earlobe, too. There's no earring, but there's a definite hole.

"So, I was pretty bitter about it at first, like my dad wasn't allowing me to fulfill my life's passion or something melodramatic like that, but I see his point now. And I can still do music on the side and be a teacher, so it all works out in the end."

That sounds logical—to choose something practical *and* follow a passion. My problem is I don't know how to do anything besides act. "That's good that it works out," I say. I want to know if he has a mother, but I don't want to be too pushy. "Did you know that you can make more money by writing and selling your songs than by performing them?"

"Really?"

"It's true. I learned that when I did *Hit the Road*. You can tell that to your dad."

"Well, that's good to know. Maybe I will." Damon turns back to the program and types SCENE 22 into a blank box. "You know, you're pretty knowledgeable about a lot of different things, Joss. You can tell that to your mother."

"Thank you." Finally, my total intelligence is starting to show. "Is that what you do after we wrap at night? Work on your music?"

"Yes, most nights. I'm also hooked on a music documentary series online. It started with fifties rock 'n' roll. I'm up to the early eighties."

"Fifties was doo-wop and jukeboxes, right? I love that time. It was so squeaky. We used to have an old man neighbor who played 'Yakety-Yak' when he cut his lawn. *Take out the papers and the trash! Or you don't get no spendin' cash!*" I sing.

"What do you mean the fifties was squeaky? Their voices? As in a mouse?"

"No. As in squeaky clean and fresh," I say. "I love poodle skirts and buttoned sweaters, and the boys slicked their hair and carried combs in their pockets . . . Hey, did you used to wear an earring?"

Damon laughs and touches his earlobe. "Yes. It got infected. I thought the post was real gold, but it wasn't, clearly. It was bad news all around." He clicks a few more keys. "Here we go. It's all set. We can get started now."

"Damon? Are you sorry you came on this adventure?" I ask.

"No way," he says, lifting my script. "I'm never sorry about an adventure."

"Me neither. I mean, I'm not sorry you came." I say. "But I have one last question."

"What's that?"

"This Live Studio thing is cool and all, but wouldn't it be easier to record the lines on my phone?" I pick up my phone off the couch and hold it up. "Plus, I can listen on my headphones and carry it around, and it'll look like I'm just listening to music."

Damon looks stunned for a second. "Uh . . . Yes. Yes, I

suppose we can do that." He laughs at himself as he closes his laptop. "I mean, if you want to be simplistic about it, sure, that'd be a different way to go."

We crack up together. We could've finished recording the scene on my phone by now.

Just then, I see Benji at our screen door holding a yellow T-shirt and some white shorts. "Sorry to interrupt, but . . ."

Our laughter ends.

Benji's very serious face tells us that my lines will have to wait. "Joss," he says, "Terrance would like to see you in his trailer."

//

TERRANCE HAS NEVER ASKED ME TO HIS TRAILER BEFORE. As far as I know, no one else has been invited there, either.

"Why does he want to see me?" I ask Benji.

He's not looking me in the eyes. "He didn't say."

Damon gives me a tight smile. "I guess we'll just have to do this later." He takes my phone and sets it on top of the script.

"Here." Benji hands me the outfit. "You can get dressed first."

In the bathroom, I peel off last night's sweats and I think of all the reasons Terrance might need to talk to me. None of the reasons are good.

I look in the mirror and see that my hair is a wreck, not just because it's supposed to be. No wonder Chris's grandma pitied me—I look like a hobo. I've got no business walking into the director's trailer like this. But what can I do? I spray the Lysol that's meant for the toilet into the air, and I walk through its mist the way Viva does with her Bath and Body Works. Hobos can't be choosers.

. . . . .

"Hey, kiddo," Terrance says slowly in a bad-news way. *Hey, kiddo, I know you're trying, but it's not good enough anymore . . .* "Come in and sit." . . . *I've noticed that you're having some trouble keeping up with the revisions. In fact, everybody's noticed . . .*

Papers are everywhere: scripts in every color, call sheets, and yellow memo pads in messy piles. I make out some random words on Post-it notes: SAFETY BOAT??!! SUNSET! FOG?? Styrofoam cups in the garbage can are mixed with banana peels and PowerBar wrappers.

"Sit down, if you can find an empty spot."

I push a space for myself on the sofa between two file boxes then sit with my hands under my thighs.

Terrance sits on the coffee table in front of me. "First off, let's clear the air, okay? Rodney told me that there might have been a little misunderstanding between you?"

I slouch deep into my seat. *Rodney told?*

"He's terribly upset about it."

Rodney told! I lift the neck hole of my T-shirt and sink my face inside it.

"He feels awful. Don't hide. You don't have to be embarrassed."

I let go of my shirt and hide behind my hand instead.

"Are you all right? Joss?"

Terrance must think I'm such a drama queen. Doris would

say that being a drama queen is definitely not pleasing on set. "I don't know what you're talking about," I mumble.

"He didn't mean to scare you. He's been wanting to apologize to you himself but felt that he might upset you even more."

Is that what Rodney was trying to do at the bonfire and also when I ran away from the schoolroom? I don't know. What if Rodney only told because he *is* a perv and was afraid I would tell first?

"He's a completely good guy. But it's important for Rodney to stay in character. I encourage it. So, this is partly my fault. I'm afraid we didn't consider that it might be a bit much for you kids. These scenes aren't easy for him, either."

Everything Terrance asks me to try, I try. Chris, too. Rodney would only do the same.

"Have you seen *Home Alone*?"

"Yes." I love *Home Alone*. I search channels for it every Christmas. It usually shows at least twice.

"Well, do you know Joe Pesci, who played the burglar? He barely talked to Macaulay Culkin the whole shoot because he wanted him to think he was really mean. And we all know how great that turned out, right?"

I did react believably in scene 15 because I was scared of Rodney in real life. I was listening to my heart, not Norah's. I understand how the whole thing works, but I still don't feel right.

"Would you like to talk with Rodney?"

"No! Nuh-uh." I squirm. I *know* how I felt with Rodney. It

didn't feel like he was pretending. And I'm supposed to follow my feelings; it's what I'm best at. But even if I'm wrong, I'm too embarrassed to face him.

"All right, then." Terrance taps my leg. "Everything's sorted."

My cheeks are burning. I just want to forget this talk ever happened. "Can I go now?"

"Not yet. Listen, Joss, there's actually another reason I called you in." He inhales and makes a teepee with his hands. I've never seen him this serious before. I knew it. He is disappointed in me.

"I know Norah doesn't like me. But I'm focused now. Really, I am," I say. "And I won't ask you about her again. I'm way too nosy. I know it's none of my business."

"No, Joss, that's not why I'm—"

"And I'm sorry I ruined the rehearsal yesterday. I won't fight anymore, I promise. I'll know all my dialogue from now on. Plus I'm getting along really good with the boys now. We were all at the bonfire. There was chicken."

"Joss, no. You're doin' great, kid. You're everything I've wanted you to be."

It must be Viva. She's pissed him off already. After all her worrying about me ruining this shoot, she's the one who's ruined it for the both of us. Or I bet his wife found out, and now we have to leave.

Terrance leans his elbows on his knees. I notice the gray hair in his sideburns. "I know that I promised you and your mother

122

that we would keep you from doing certain scenes," he says very slowly.

This is even worse than I thought. Much worse. It's the worst.

"But I need just a little something more. So, last night I rewrote scene twenty. It's exactly what's been missing. If you do this for me, the film will be perfect."

Don't you dare freak out, I hear Viva's voice saying in my head. But I shut her out because this time she's wrong. She's so, so, so wrong.

"No, Terrance. No!" It's the first time I've ever said no to a director. But he's wrong, too, and Rodney is still so, so, so scary. I don't want to play scenes about getting molested.

"It's not a physical scene, Joss. Rodney isn't even *in* it. It's only dialogue between Norah and TJ. I promise."

"But you already promised months ago." I don't hold back because I'm right. And if my mother said no to something it must be terrible. "You were going to shoot that stuff around me. Chris was going to have lines about it, not me. You *know* it, Terrance. My mother said I'm not allowed."

"I've already spoken with Viva," Terrance says as if it's as good as done. "She understands and said it's okay. Hey, how about when we're done, we'll go to the lighthouse? Just the three of us."

I back away. There's no way to make this up to me.

"You already spoke to her?" I ask. He spoke to my mother first because she's screwing him, so he knew she'd take his side.

And then she asked Terrance to tell me so that I wouldn't have a choice.

If Viva isn't on my side, who is?

"I can't do the scene, Terrance." I reach for the most professional argument I have. "My agent called Peter Bustamante. My contract *says*—"

"I know. I'm so sorry." Terrance stares at the floor.

There aren't enough sorrys for this.

Don't you dare cry. Don't you dare. He'll have to call action before he ever sees a tear from me.

"It's the film, Joss. I've been over it and over it, and it's not the story I need it to be yet. Norah has to at least tell TJ about the abuse. It has to come from her. She has to . . . she has to be that strong."

But why should I have to?

"I really need you for this, kiddo. Please." He pulls the rolled-up scene out of his back pocket and uncurls it—the paper is blue.

The blue script was four revisions ago.

"You've had that scene from the *beginning*." I point at the pages. "You've just been keeping it from me."

It's Terrance's life story. Of course the scene was there from the start like the crow's nest and the fight. That scene's been there for thirty years.

"No, no. It's brand-new," he lies straight to my face. "I called you right in to talk to you about it. The copies aren't even done yet."

I push as far back from him as I can. I don't want him talking to me anymore, not ever again. When I look down at myself, I'm in white shorts and a yellow T-shirt I don't recognize. And I smell funny, too, like a toilet brush.

I'm disappearing little by little . . .

On the end table, with papers and maps and receipts, there's a small envelope sealed with a seashell sticker. It's the letter I wrote to Norah. I remember the address Terrance gave me and the note Damon helped me write. Norah Rivenbach, 47 Skipped Rock Rd., Montauk, NY.

> *Dear Norah,*
> *I would love to meet you. Please*
> *visit our set soon!*
>
> > *Love,*
> > *Joss Byrd*

"You're my muse, you know that, don't you, kid?" Terrance says, as if that still means something special. "I would've done anything, anything to have you be my Norah."

Including lie to me.

Norah said, *"You don't want to be his sister. You don't even want to know him."*

"You have today to work on it. We'll shoot it tomorrow night after the drive-thru deli. That way you can get it over with. The winds will be low. It'll be a nice night out on the beach."

You can't put a night shoot together in one day. He had to reserve the beach and check the winds ahead of time.

"She hates a lot of things," Terrance said.

When Terrance came up behind me, she narrowed her eyes at him—her eyes were sad from being the real Norah.

Norah doesn't hate *me*. She hates *Terrance*. That's what's in Norah's heart.

"I think that once you read it," Terrance says, "you'll see that it's not a big deal, really. It's nothing at all."

Thinking back to Terrance's big, warm hug on that first day, I agree. "Nothing at all."

He gives me the script. It rolls up again in my hands as if it's ashamed of itself. And it should be.

"That's my girl." Terrance pats me like I'm a dog. But really, he should be patting himself on the back for getting away with this.

12

AS FAST AS I CAN, I'M RUNNING PAST WARDROBE RACKS that are packed with faded jeans; the hair and makeup trailer blasting dance music; the old, graying dog that's sitting in the truck driver's passenger seat; and Rodney stepping out of Peter Bustamante's trailer.

"Hey, Norah!" Rodney yells after me. "Where are you going? Did you talk to TJ?"

I whip around, fists clenched. "My name is *Joss*! And you can stay away from me!" I scream because I can't believe anything Terrance says anymore.

My dressing room door swings open behind me. "What is going on out here? Joss?" Viva says.

I take off again, even faster. My mother is the last person I want to see, and basecamp is the last place I want to be.

"Ray?" I call, spotting him and his friends at the far end of the parking lot on their dirt bikes.

"Hi!" he says as he rolls his bicycle toward me.

"Do you know where Skipped Rock Road is?" Until that came out of my mouth I didn't know what I was going to say. But Norah's the only one who might understand. Maybe she'll be on my side. "I need to get to 47 Skipped Rock Road."

"Sure, I know where it is," Ray says as his friends stare at me. "Get on." He taps his handlebars. "I can take you."

I shove my script in my back pocket and hop on. The handlebar digs into my butt as I balance my toes on the bolts of Ray's front wheel.

"Are you on a secret mission? Like research for your character or something?" Ray steers and presses his flip-flopped feet over the pedals.

"Something like that."

"I knew it! So cool."

"Joss! Where are you going?" I hear Benji yell from the parking lot. "You're still in school! You already owe two hours! You're about to owe three!"

"Montauk's a small town," Ray says as we speed through the streets. "But we have a real good time here. That's probably why they film so many movies here."

The breeze hits my face when we turn the corner, and we're coasting downhill. I almost forget why I'm riding away. If I were a regular kid, just one of the locals, I'd be woo-hooing from on top of Ray's bike. A part of me is having a grand time, the same part of me that can't remember the last time I had real fun.

"Which number again?" Ray asks when we get to Skipped

Rock Road, but I can't think of it. I can only think of Norah and Terrance and Rodney. Suddenly I'm the dirt driveway kid who's pretending to be an actor.

But I don't have to remember the house number because Norah is on her front lawn throwing weeds into a paper bag.

"That's her," I say. "I can get off here."

Ray plants his feet on the ground. "I'll wait right here for you."

I hop down but hold the handlebar for a second before letting go.

Norah leaves the paper bag on the grass. She walks up to me wearing her gardening gloves. She doesn't seem surprised in the least to see me. As she gets closer, I see little lines at the corners of her eyes, and the freckles on her nose are the same as mine when I get too much sun. But it's our chins that are most alike, with a slight dent in the middle.

"Hello, Joss. What is it?" She takes her gloves off. "Are you okay?"

"You were right. I don't even want to know him." I go to pull the script from my pocket but decide not to. I'm not sure why. "He promised I wouldn't have to do something, but he lied."

"Well." Norah takes a deep breath. "Considering everything else he's done, I'm not surprised."

"What did he do?"

"He's making this movie in the first place," she says, almost laughing. "Isn't that enough?"

I remember sweaty Rodney. I didn't want anyone but Chris to know he came into my schoolroom. Of course Norah doesn't want the whole world to know that horrible stuff happened to her. That's why I don't want to show her the script. Norah's not just a character I have to play. She was once a girl who got abused by her stepdad. Norah's a living person with feelings.

How can Terrance do this to her?

How can I?

"He says that we each have to deal with our lives in our own way and that I have my way and he has his." She smacks her gloves against her thigh. "But that just means he doesn't care how it affects me."

I don't want to be in this movie anymore. I was so blind. I thought it was better to be anyone but me and that it would actually be fun to play Norah Rivenbach. I couldn't wait to be Chris's sister and Terrance's star. I've got guilt so thick right now that I can barely see through it.

"Five years ago when he started writing the screenplay, I thought, fine. It'll be therapeutic for him. He'll get it all out of his system. But as soon as he told me he was actually going to make the movie? That was it for me. That's not the brother I know. He's had tunnel vision ever since." Norah drops her gloves and leads me to the stoop where we have a seat. It feels good to sit. I'm tired, but I didn't know it. "*The Locals* has been all he can think about: casting the perfect kids, searching for the same kind of crappy boat, even finding a place with the perfect *tree*. Hell, he's even had the nerve to call me in the middle of the night, on several occasions, to make sure he had the dialogue exactly right." She wipes her forehead. "I told him that since he's the one who likes remembering, he could figure it out himself."

"I'm sorry, Norah." It's not enough, but I don't know what else to say.

"Don't be. None of this is about you."

But it is about me. I've been acting out her secrets for a lobster dinner.

I watch Norah roll her sleeves over her elbows. "If he has to make the movie, I'm glad that he cast you and not someone else."

"Why?" I can't think of a single reason.

She reaches over, pulls one yellow daisy from the flower bed, and offers it to me. "Because you are sorry. And if you don't do it someone else will, probably some shallow Hollywood kid whose face is on lunch boxes and sleeping bags. At least TJ got one thing right."

I don't want to accept the flower. I wanted her to like me so bad, but now, playing Norah isn't right. And I don't want to feel her emotions anymore; there's too much of them to feel. But I take the daisy from her anyway—how can I say no?

Over my shoulder, I can see through Norah's front door, straight through her tidy living room, and all the way through her sliding glass doors. In the backyard, there's a tall, wide tree in the exact center of—

I can't believe it. This must be the house—the one Norah and Terrance grew up in. I can picture them here when they were young, screaming and fighting with their stepdad. This place is its own kind of haunted house. Why would she still want to live here?

· · · · ·

As we turn into the Beverly Hills neighborhood, my mother slows the rental car and turns the radio down. She doesn't care to visit Disneyland or Universal Studios or the beach. For our first time in LA, she wants to see rich-people houses. Now I know why. The Disney castle can't beat this.

I don't know which house to look at first. One has got bushes that look like giant Q-tips leading all the way up the driveway. Another has rounded balconies outside every bedroom. Across the way there's a shiny, old-fashioned black car; the wheel spokes sparkle like jewelry.

"Holy moly," my mother whispers.

I fold my arms over the car window and rest my chin on my hands. We pass a bright blue door with a thick brass knocker. If I run up there and knock, would they let me in or would they laugh me away?

Viva gasps at the house with the vines up the side. "Look at all the ivy. Old Hollywood." She tucks her hair into her floppy sun hat and checks her lipstick in the mirror. "I could fit in here, couldn't I?"

We'd both get laughed away. But it'd be mean to tell her so.

"You see? Now this is where I'm meant to live. Right here. In the 9-0-2-1-0." She stops the car to take a picture of herself in front of a house with a fountain. "We're on our way, Joss. Can you feel it?" She drives slowly, watching her dream house roll by. "We're on our way."

My mother says we. *But I know that it's all up to me.*

. . . . .

"Norah, is this . . . the house?" I ask, afraid of my own question. "The one you lived in as a kid?"

"Yes. It is." She smiles as she turns to look through the door.

"Oh . . ." I keep imagining the hitting and crying and worse that happened inside years ago when the house was shabby. "Well, you fixed it up nice," I say. It's not my business to tell her she's crazy for living with those bad memories, but one thing I've learned for sure is that there's always someplace better.

"It's not much different than when we were young." Norah brushes the hair off her face. "I just keep up with it, that's all."

"You mean . . ." The clean windows are opened up to the breeze, and neat bricks line the flower bed. There's even a real driveway, solid and everything. "You weren't *poor*?" I ask, shocked.

Norah looks at the houses across the street. One is very narrow but it's been built up to three stories. "We weren't living it up like some families here, but no. We weren't *poor*."

"But that house we're filming in . . ." No wonder Terrance doesn't mind showing that he was poor—because it isn't true! Well, he sure had me fooled. He had me, my mother, Christopher, the whole cast and crew fooled. And when the movie comes out, he'll have Hollywood fooled, too.

"Yeah. What a joke, right?" Norah stands and pulls a weed from the grass. "I heard the address. But I assumed they'd fix it up, put some movie magic into it. But no." She throws the weed into the paper bag. "That's TJ, though. He knows what makes for a better movie. It's just too bad he can't rewrite my entire childhood."

I understand what she means. The house was rewritten, but the awful parts about her and Rodney are true.

"But, Norah?" There's still something I want to know; I can't let it go. "Why do you *stay* here?" I look up at her from where I'm sitting, shielding my eyes from the sun.

"The ocean," she says, as if it's so obvious.

"Hello there!" A man holding a babbling chubby baby steps out of the house. "You're Joss, aren't you?"

"Yes. Hello."

"I'm Henry, Norah's husband. And this is Pearl." He holds Pearl's arm out so that I can shake her soft little hand.

"Hey, Pearl. I'm Joss. Nice to meet you."

Henry adjusts Pearl's white sailor hat. "Sunny today, isn't it?" He lays a blanket on the grass and sets Pearl on it. She sits up unsteadily, grabbing her toes.

"It's so nice of you to come visit us."

I'm glad for Norah. Henry is calm and kind. He's the very opposite of her evil stepdad.

"Can I get you a lemonade or an iced tea?" he asks, and I like him even more.

"No, thank you. I can't stay."

Norah kneels to play with Pearl. "I was just telling Joss the great things about living in our house."

"Well, that's easy." Henry gives Pearl a pacifier. "Montauk's beautiful. We can see the shoreline from out back."

"We built a crow's nest," Norah says.

All's we need now is a pair of binoculars. Then we can see clear through to the lighthouse . . . one of those old-timey pirate telescopes that stretch . . . If we get one of those, we'll have it made. We'll be the luckiest kids in Montauk . . .

Rodney may have ruined the crow's nest when Norah and Terrance were kids, but he couldn't stop Norah from building it when she grew up. I guess there are lots of ways to rewrite your life.

"Bah-bah-bah!" The baby is reaching her arms out toward Ray's bicycle.

"She's obsessed with bikes." Henry picks Pearl up and walks toward Ray. "You want to see the big boy bike?" Henry holds the baby on the bicycle seat. She looks so happy blowing spit bubbles and clapping while Ray makes motorcycle noises and pretends to steer the handlebars.

If I do scene 20 will that make me weak, or will that make me brave? If I don't, will I be a quitter or hero?

"What will you do, Norah?" I ask, hoping to find my answer in hers.

"I'm suing my brother and the producer, or I'm trying to—for using my name and my image without my permission," she says.

"You are?" I ask proudly. Now that is scrappy. "Then you'll get your brother's money and he'll have to live in that shack for real."

"No way." Norah laughs. "I'm not going to win, Joss."

"Why not?"

"Because, aside from the pitiful house, the story's true. I don't have much of a case if it's true. And besides, my brother isn't TJ anymore. He's *Terrance Rivenbach*." Norah lifts her hand as if she's reading his name on a movie screen.

For some reason, I remember Bella Pratt and her smart-aleck friends back at school. There are bullies everywhere.

"Then why are you even trying?" I ask.

Norah crosses her arms and pinches her elbow. "Because he didn't think I would. And if I don't stand up for myself, nobody will."

And what about me? What should I do? I want to ask Norah. But I don't. She's got enough of her own weeds to pull.

I should get back to basecamp. If I don't, Benji will have a panic attack about my schooling hours. When I turn back to

Ray it's obvious he's overheard everything. Does this answer his question about what it's like to be an actor?

"Bah-bah-bah!" Pearl coos.

Suddenly, here's Benji running up the road. He's come to take me back. Fetch Joss. As soon as Benji spots me, he collapses, hands on his knees. "I found her." He pants into his walkie-talkie. "I got the Bessie."

⋅ ⋅ ⋅ ⋅ ⋅

In my schooling trailer, Viva and Damon are looking at me sideways like they're visiting me in a nut house. I keep my back to my mother while I dial my phone. If she won't do it, I'll have to fix this myself. But Viva isn't even trying to stop me; she's just watching quietly as if she knows what to expect.

"Creative Team Management," says the voice on the other end. "Doris Cole here."

"Doris?" My voice breaks. "I don't want to do this anymore." I pull the crunched script from my pocket and throw it on the table. "It's just bad here, really bad. The real Norah doesn't even want Terrance to do this movie. Neither do I. They're making me . . . they're making me do an abuse scene!"

"Joss, calm down, honey."

"They can't do this, right?" I beg. "I'm too young for any of that. You wrote it up in my *contract*."

"Now, now. I've read the scene," she says, easy breezy. "Everything's gonna be fine. I hear that you're doing a bang-up job out there. I'm so proud of you. Everyone in the office is proud of you, even Tubsy-ubsy. She says meow! She's right here . . . aren't you, Tubsy? Production is happy. Everybody's happy. So you just finish out what they tell you to do, and it's all gonna be—"

I hang up on Doris as I spin around with tears in my eyes. "Mommy!"

"Don't, Joss. Don't you dare cry," my mother says, fighting a tremble in her own voice. "Don't you dare turn diva on me. Now you just sit down and you learn it."

"You *promised* me. You said that Norah had it really bad and that we were drawing the line," I say, shaking.

"Oh, don't be so dramatic." She turns her back and spreads her fingers on the door. "Show the script to Damon. Learn it."

13

DAMON TAKES HIS SEAT. WE LISTEN TO THE FAUCET DRIPPING in the bathroom, the air conditioner whirring, and someone outside dumping a cooler of ice onto the blacktop. A wardrobe rack wheels past my door. My phone vibrates. I throw it into my backpack.

"I'm really sorry that you have to do this," Damon says.

Don't. You. Dare. Cry.

He takes a package of Twix candy bars from his pocket and slides it toward me. I flick the crumpled, rolled-up script across the table at Damon. We stare at it like it's a stick of dynamite.

"Maybe it isn't that bad?" he asks. "I'm just gonna read it aloud, okay? I'll do it fast, like ripping off a Band-Aid."

I lay my head on my arms and hear him separating the pages.

"So. It looks like three pages . . . just you and Christopher." Damon clears his throat.

At least that much is true—no Rodney. Maybe it'll be all right.

Damon reads, emotionless. It's like he's reading instructions on how to assemble a toy:

[At night. Norah runs through the path
toward the beach. She is soaking wet in
a T-shirt and shorts. TJ spots her as
she bursts through the clearing. He
chases her, calling her name. Norah
reaches the sand. She collapses at the
foot of the dunes, shivering, panting.]

TJ: Norah? God, you're soaking.
        You're shivering. What happened?

[Norah hugs her knees, rocks back and
forth.]

Norah: I can't . . . I can't say it.

TJ: It was him, wasn't it? He did
        something to you?

[He takes off his flannel shirt and
wraps it around his sister.]

Norah: Don't make me go back there, TJ,
        please. I can't go back there.

TJ: We won't. We won't. I promise.
         But you have to tell me, Norah.
         You have to. What did he do?

Norah: He was in the shower, and he
         was yelling for me to get him
         a towel. He kept yelling and
         screaming that when I do the
         laundry I have to replace the
         goddamn towels.

Damon's voice starts to shake a little, giving away what we
both knew from the start—it really *is* that bad.

*"You got it! You got it! You got it!" my mother is screeching through
the house. She picks me up off the floor in front of the television
and jumps up and down. I'm still holding my spoon and my cereal
bowl. Milk and Froot Loops fly into the air and land all over the
room as my mother swings me around.*

"You're Tallulah Leigh! You did it! You got the part!"

*And now we're both laughing from being hit so hard with so
much luck.*

*Tallulah Leigh! Tallulah Leigh! I say the name in my head to
make it mine.*

*"They said you have sad eyes, deep as bat caves!" my mother says
happily. I don't know why it's good to have bat-cave eyes, but if
she's glad about them, so am I. Then, in her holey sleep clothes and*

with one fat roller in her bangs, she runs outside to our neighbors'
yard. "Joss is gonna be in a movie! We're going to Hollywood!"

Anything that can make my mother this proud of me must be a
miracle. While she hugs our neighbors I twirl behind her in my
nightshirt, pretending it's a ball gown. Each time she says "Holly-
wood!" I picture my mother wearing big sunglasses, her hair in a
scarf, and driving a convertible. Because of me she'll get to be the
glamorous lady she's always wanted to be. Hollywood! will always
be sunny. We'll never need to put the top up!

· · · · ·

". . . And that's it," Damon says softly. "Sorry. I don't mean that's
it, I just mean, that's all there is."

I hold tears behind my eyes and stare at the Twix.

"We'll record it now, okay?" He reaches for my backpack.

"No. No recording."

Damon touches my elbow. "It's okay, Joss. I'll go ahead and
read both parts for this one."

"No, Damon. I already know it."

When dynamite explodes in your ear, you don't forget it.

"Oh, okay . . . well, good. Do you want to just run through
it, then?"

I shake my head. "Thank you, but can you please get
Chris for me?" For some reason, saying Chris's name pushes
full, heavy tears from my eyes. "I'll just practice it with him,
okay?"

142

"Yes, of course. I think that's a really good idea." He rips a paper towel from the roll and hands it to me. "I'll go find him."

. . . . .

I'm full-on crying by the time Chris comes in. He sits beside me without talking while I let out everything that I've been holding in.

"Terrance has gray hair—*gray*. He's an *adult*. He can do whatever he wants. He doesn't have to do what other people tell him to anymore. Why would he want to remember any of this? Why doesn't he just move on already?"

"I don't know . . . I don't know . . ." is all Chris keeps saying, real quiet-like.

I blubber into the scratchy paper towel. "Why can't he just forget about it?"

"I don't know . . ."

"Why can't he drop it, for Norah?" I say. "I went to see her. She isn't mad at me. It's Terrance. She wants to sue him. She told me herself. She doesn't want him filming *The Locals*."

"What?" He grabs the top of his head. "Sheesh . . ."

I rip another towel off the roll. "You're supposed to move on and not look back."

"He should." Chris nods. "He really should."

"I don't want to do it, Chris. I don't want to say those things." I cover my face.

"Everyone's gonna know it really happened to Norah.

143

And she has a baby; when she gets older, she's gonna know, too."

"That's not your fault. That's Terrance's fault," he says. "Hey, it's hard for me to play TJ, too. Like, every time he tells me how sad, how pissed, how hurt my character is, it's weird because I know he's talking about himself."

"But he wants everyone to know about his childhood. Norah doesn't. And getting hit is different than getting . . . getting . . ." I can't even say the word here in my trailer. How can I act on camera like I've been molested? "And everyone's gonna . . . remember me . . . like that . . . for the rest of my life." I hiccup between sobs.

"You're right. They will," Chris says. It's surprising how plain and simple the truth sounds. Because of *Camp Magaskawee*, no matter what other roles Chris plays, people still remember him having diarrhea against a tree. And Doris says I'll always be known for the parts I'm doing now. It was the same for Tatum O'Neal and *Paper Moon*. But I don't want to be remembered as a poor, abused girl. I want to be happy and light and beautiful.

"There's always crap parts of a movie. For me, literally, there were crap parts," Chris says. "But you know what else I got on that movie? I got a motorized car that I rode around the lot all month, and when we wrapped I asked to take it home, and they shipped it to my house the next day."

I bet he ripped that big box open right on his doorstep.

"So this scene is the crap part of *The Locals*. But after

144

tomorrow, it's all cake, right? We get *surf* lessons!" He shakes my arm. "*Surf* lessons! We get to shoot our last scene in the ocean while every other kid on Earth is sitting in a classroom. How sweet is that?"

"Pretty sweet." I try hard to see past tomorrow. I try to imagine the first seconds of diving into the cool ocean.

"Tomorrow we'll be TJ and Norah for Terrance and Peter and our families, but then we can celebrate because everything left is all for *us*. Who knows? Maybe we'll nail this in one take and that'll be that."

"Right." That would be impossible.

"How 'bout this?" Chris's voice lightens. "I buy a surfboard for you and you buy one for me."

I wipe my nose. In the surf shop there's a blue board with yellow flowers on it, a Hawaiian pattern. I've had my eye on it since we got here.

"We'll give 'em to each other at the wrap party."

I'd like that. I imagine tiki torches at the party. For some reason, I've always wanted to be at a party where there's tiki torches. If only Terrance didn't have to be there. Or my mother. Or Rodney.

"I told off Rodney," I say.

Chris looks at me like I'm nuts. *"You did?"*

"I know I shouldn't have. He's a grown-up, our costar. He'll be even angrier at me now." I exhale into my hands. "Oh, I don't know . . ." I wish I knew once and for all if Rodney is bad or good so that I can be sorry or not. "Plus, everyone heard. They probably all think I'm a diva. I was just so mad."

Chris holds his hands up. "Hey, you don't have to explain it to me."

"Viva's freaking."

"She's always freaking. So's Rodney. That's their problem."

"Hey, Chris?" I ask, remembering something I've been wondering all day. "What's a Bessie? I heard Terrance and Benji call me one."

"What is wrong with people? Doesn't anyone keep anything to themselves anymore?" Chris pauses with his eyes down before blurting, "It's a prized calf. A cash cow."

"I'm . . . a *cow*?" In my mind I see Terrance selling me for magic beans.

"A Bessie is someone who makes her owners lots of money."

Terrance plants his seeds. Then they grow into a giant beanstalk. He climbs it up through the clouds to his castle in the sky.

"Hey, hey. This is what you do, okay?" Chris touches my arm. "If you're the Bessie, then *be* the Bessie."

"Huh?"

"Kick ass on camera. The better you are, the bigger Bessie you can be. That means the more demands you can make. Production will have to give you anything you want."

What would I do with a motorized car? "But I don't want anything." Except not to do scene 20 to begin with.

"You will. Trust me," he says, confidently. "Eventually, everybody wants something."

146

"I guess." I pick the script up. We might as well get this over with.

"No. Let's not practice it today." He takes the rolled-up pages and sets them on the seat beside him. "We'll rehearse tomorrow after the deli scene. That way we'll only have one bad night."

That sounds all right to me.

"You guys have Jenga?" he asks, eyeing the game in the corner.

"Damon brought it. He thought we'd have tons of free time."

"Do you have anything else today besides school?" Chris has a glimmer in his eyes.

"Just a bathing suit fitting after lunch."

"Good." He gets up to open the trailer door. "Excuse me, Damon? We're gonna need at least an hour," he says. Then he turns back inside and points to the floor. "Well, go on. Set it up!"

So I pour the game pieces. We crisscross and stack the smooth wooden blocks higher and higher into a perfect column, and then steady as we can, we pull blocks out one by one and replace them carefully on the top. I want to get into the game; it'd be fun on a regular day. But now it's just another thing I can't stop from crashing down.

14

"WE CAN CLIMB THROUGH THE DRIVE-THRU WINDOW!"
Chris says, running full-speed around the Milk-n-Stuff deli.

Me and Jericho are on his tail, kicking up dust as we go like
in a cartoon. Out of the corner of my eye I see my mother
(what nerve!), standing close to Terrance (on the job!) behind
the camera.

Terrance has been directing this morning as if nothing's
changed between us. He isn't sorry at all about the talk we had
yesterday, which is even worse than going back on a promise.
He also isn't the least bit embarrassed by Viva. He's whispering
in her ear with his hand on her back when he should be back-
ing away and pointing her toward the monitors where the
parents are supposed to be.

Jericho grabs the windowsill. "Lift me through! I'm goin' in!"
he yells. "Toss me over!"

"No. I don't trust you in there." Chris pulls me in front of him.
I nearly stumble over my own feet. "We're sending Norah in."

"Yes! Yes!" I jump up and down. "I can do it! Let me!" I'm saying the words but am too distracted to feel them because my mother and Terrance are out in the open daylight, looking very cozy, as if they're a couple. A couple of backstabbers is what they are.

"What do you guys want? Cookies? Apple caramels?" I look from Chris to Jericho.

"Cut!" Terrance yells. "Joss, you said apple caramels instead of caramel apples."

"No, I didn't," I say. At least, I'm pretty sure I didn't.

"No worries." Terrance lifts his hand. "Just watch your lines. It has to be exactly right."

"I know the lines. I know every single one." What a laugh this is: after recording the dialogue on my phone and memorizing it the way me and Damon planned, I finally do know all the words, but now I can't concentrate.

"Don't talk back, Joss." Viva steps forward in her platform sandals. "He didn't say you didn't *know* them. He said *watch* them."

She should be minding her own business. It's bad enough they've teamed up against me. Do they have to do it in front of everybody?

"We'll go again, okay?" Terrance says. "From Joss's 'Yes, yes.'"

While Jericho peers through the drive-thru window, I mumble under my breath to Chris. "I can't take them anymore,

I mean it. If my mother pokes her nose in scene twenty to-night, I'll never be able to do it."

"Don't think about tonight," Chris whispers. "This is all we're doing right now, so keep your head in it, okay?"

"Hey! There are Mallomars in there! I haven't had those since, like, second grade!" Jericho says.

The Milk-n-Stuff is like a junk-food pit stop on the way to heaven. It would normally be my new favorite place. But today, before the worse scene ever, this set is just sweet and fake, like everything else on *The Locals*.

"Grab me a box of those when you get in there, will you, Joss?" Jericho asks. "I love it when we get to eat the props."

Is that the only thing missing in Jericho's charmed life? *Mallomars?*

"Get 'em yourself," I grumble.

"Roll sound! Rolling!" Terrance calls, with his hands resting on top of his head. "And . . . action!"

"Yes! Yes!" I clap and hop on the balls of my feet. "I can do it! Let me! What do you guys want? Cookies? Caramel apples? I'll even get you those gross jerky things!"

Did I say it right?

"Why her?" Jericho asks. Suddenly I can't remember what he's talking about, and I have to tell myself to listen, feel, react.

"Because she'll stay out of the cash register and the dirty magazines," Chris says, reminding me where we are.

Jericho groans. "Okay." He sticks his finger in my face while

I try to figure out how to react. "But you'd better get me some hot dogs or I'm going in after you."

Now my mother is holding her phone up to the monitor, probably to show me later how bad I was. Taking video during shooting probably isn't allowed. There's got to be a rule somewhere. But who's gonna say no to Viva when she's partners in crime with Terrance?

"I will. Now, boost me!" I face the drive-thru and grip the ledge. I'm glad to turn my back on Terrance and my mother.

When Chris links his fingers together to make a step, I put my foot in and push myself up by balancing on Jericho's shoulder.

"Be careful on the other side," Chris says.

"I got it, I got it. Hold your horses."

The ledge has been padded so that I won't skin myself as I wriggle my belly over it. I spot a thick gymnastics mat on the deli floor, swing my left leg up, and climb over.

"Cut!" Terrance laughs.

I land softly on the mat and bounce.

"Good, kids. Really good."

Compliments from Terrance irritate me now because: 1) the scene wasn't any good at all, so he must be blind; 2) I don't want to impress him anymore; 3) LIAR!!!

"Let's get a few more," I hear Terrance say as I walk through the store. I spot the Mallomars on the shelf and leave them there. "More energy for the next one, all right? Remember you're supposed to be hungry, and this is a store full of goodies! Let's reset."

As soon as I step out of the door, Viva bursts out laughing as if she was holding it in the whole scene. "Do you think you can do that just a little bit more gracefully, Joss?" She holds her phone up to show me. "You have to see this video. It's hilarious—your butt hanging over the edge in those shorts!"

What's there to laugh at? Eating too much and growing too tall and zits and training bras and my butt aren't things to joke about. Definitely not in front of my cast and my crew. I'm so mad I can understand how Oscar Coombs could smash a camera.

Chris shakes his head and mouths at me to stay focused.

I shuffle the gravel on my way toward Damon. "Did you *hear* her?" I ask him.

"I heard it," Damon says. "I saw the whole thing."

"I need some air," I say, which might sound stupid because we're already outside, but it's true. "I have to take a walk or something. They're resetting the camera."

"Sure. Let's power walk, burn off some steam. That'll be good." He motions to Benji where we're going.

We take a wide lap around the deli. It's more peaceful on the woodsy side where there isn't any crew, but our porta potty smack-dab between the trees ruins the view.

I pump my arms faster when we turn the corner and my mother is back in sight. "I hate her, Damon."

"Don't say that. She's still your mom," he says, lifting imaginary dumbbells.

Copying him, I pretend to lift dumbbells, too. We should count this as PE for school. "No. I do. I really do hate her."

"Stop. You don't mean that. Plus, your mic might still be on," he reminds me.

I touch the mic pack that's clipped inside the back of my shorts. If Viva heard me, then so what? If she wants me to love her she should be more lovable. And if the crew heard me, and they're surprised to learn that America's sweetheart hates her mother, they'll get over it. Believe me: images get shattered every day.

Damon checks over his shoulder. "Let's keep walking until they call you back. Break a sweat. It's healthy for you. And do yourself a favor. Try to think about something positive for a few minutes."

. . . . .

"Is this real marble?" I ask, sitting on the cool bathroom counter.

"I think so." Viva dusts over my eyelids with a tiny makeup brush. "But if it isn't, we could demand that the manager bring us some more chocolate-covered strawberries."

"It's so clean." I slide my palms across the sparkly white surface. "How do they chip marble into sculptures with nothing but a screwdriver thingy and that little hammer?"

"Oh, gosh, how would I know? I can barely use the self-serve frozen yogurt machine."

I giggle as I bite into my sixth strawberry. Usually it's gross to eat in a bathroom. But in a Hollywood hotel on Oscar night when your movie is nominated for Best Picture, it's considered fancy.

"There, all set. You. Look. Gorge." My mother bounces the blush brush on my nose. She looks pretty, too. Her hair is wavy like she's in a movie from the Golden Age. "Now, for the best part—our shoes!" She claps and hurries into the bedroom. "Joss! Come quick! Look! Look what's on!" she calls. I hop off the counter and run after her, carrying the silver tray with the rest of the strawberries.

Live from the Red Carpet is on the TV, and the host is talking about Buy One, Get One.

"This quiet, sleeper hit costarring the little powerhouse, America's darling, Joss Byrd . . ." Suddenly my picture, a still photo from Buy One, Get One, *flashes on the screen.*

"Powerhouse!" we squeal. "America's darling!" I set the strawberries on the dresser. Then we jump up and down on the bed, designer dresses and all.

· · · · ·

I'm a little out of breath by the time we're ready to roll again. This is what happens when you miss months of gym class. Back at the drive-thru, I curl my fingers over the windowsill to get my mind back into the scene.

"You all right?" Chris asks, taking his mark beside me. "You're all sweaty."

"Yeah, I'm all right." I roll my shoulders and wait for my

pulse to slow down. "You know how you said that eventually everybody wants something?" I ask.

"Yeah . . ." He lowers his face, curious.

"Well, I know what I want now." I lift my chin confidently. "And it's not a motorized car."

15

BENJI STOCKED MY TRAILER WITH MICROWAVE POPCORN, fizzy lemonade in glass bottles, and candy from the shop down the road—handmade local fudge. He called them "delectables." It's so obvious that these freebies are supposed to keep me happy—happy enough to do a scene I don't want to do. I'd get anything I asked for right now, like an ice-cream sundae or a chocolate croissant from the bakery in town. Since the only thing I really want is to scrap this scene altogether and that's impossible, I at least want to get through it without worrying about what my mother will do or say or think of me. In order to get that I need to do as Chris said: be the Bessie.

Tatum O'Neal's close-up is on my screen. She's scrappy as any kid can be with her eyes squinted and her jaw set. I stare at her and then I stare at her some more so that I can work up my own courage. When Tatum clenches her fist, I copy her. Then I pound on the table with my elbow bent. I press pause to make the same face in the mirror—eyes narrow, lips tight.

I can do this. I can do this. I can do this.

Opening the door to my dressing trailer, I call for Benji. "I want to talk to Peter Bustamante," I say. It's my biggest line so far.

Benji wrinkles his brow. "Peter?" Benji might be used to bringing me breakfast and clothes, but he's never brought me the executive producer before.

"Yes, please," I say surely.

He nods. "I'll let him know, Miss Byrd."

The lumps of local fudge are labeled Bit of Heaven. The waxy wrapper peels right off.

Sweet. Also salty.

One more for good measure. I know I said I didn't want the fudge, but it doesn't hurt. A bit of bravery.

I unfreeze Tatum on my laptop so that she can yell at her father to give her the money he owes her.

"But I don't *have* it," her father says.

Tatum stares him down. Tough as nails, she says, "Then *get* it!"

"Get it!" I yell at my reflection.

"Joss?" Peter knocks. He's here much quicker than I expected. "You wanted to talk to me?"

I pause the DVD and take a second before letting him in. "Get it," I whisper to myself.

Peter barely steps both feet into the trailer before I open my mouth. "I don't want my mother here for this scene," I blurt, while I've got the nerve. "She's outside talking to Terrance. I want you to tell her to go."

He leans against the counter. "But Joss, she's your mother."

"She can come back tomorrow. But not this scene. It's bad enough she's making me do this. She doesn't have to direct it, too. She messed me up at the drive-thru deli. She was nothing but a distraction, a colossal embarrassment. I barely got through that scene. She'll mess me up again if she's here. This is my big moment, Peter," I say, remembering how Terrance talked me into scene 15. If there was a way to ban him from being here, I'd do that, too. "You want me to do it right, don't you?"

"Joss, you know you have to have a guardian on set."

"I asked someone else, who'll be here any second. Please, tell my mother to go."

Peter scratches his stubble. "Viva isn't going to like this, Joss."

"Well, you don't have to do what Viva wants. You have to do what *I* want." I pound my fist and squint. "*I'm* the Bessie, aren't I?"

That stops Peter in his tracks. He blinks at me, surprised.

I give him my stoniest expression. "Tell her she isn't allowed here."

"Okay . . . okay." He nods. "As long as you have someone else."

That very second, as if we practiced it, there's a tap-tap-tap. I'm proud to open the door to let Norah in. I'm even prouder at how prepared she is—windbreaker, canteen on a strap—the ideal night shoot uniform. I keep my eye on Peter as Norah hugs me. I want to catch the shock on his face.

"Norah?" Peter says. "What are you . . . how did you . . . how are you?"

Norah holds her shoulders back. "How do you think I am, Buzz?"

Buzz? Peter Bustamante? That's where the name came from? I had no idea. Norah's fight is twice as hard as I thought.

"Look," Peter says, "I know this whole thing has been difficult for you—"

"Difficult? Is that what you call stealing my shitty childhood and calling it entertainment?"

"I'm sorry it went down this way, Norah."

"Then don't film the scene, Buzz. Not this one."

"It's not my call."

"Yes, it is. You're the only one who can talk some sense into him at this point. You grew up with us. You know what I went through. How can you sell me out for ten dollars a ticket?"

I lean against the wall and try to remember that this isn't my fault; if it wasn't me, it'd be some other girl. But I can't fool myself. Even if it isn't my fault, it will still be my picture on the movie poster, selling those tickets.

"Everything's ready to go," Peter says. "TJ's hyped up. You know how he gets. I can't stop it, Norah. It's TJ's set."

"But it's my *life*, Buzz!" Norah is staring him down. "If you can't stop him now, cut the scene later. Edit it out. You can do that much for me, can't you?" she pleads. "You were my friend as much as you were TJ's."

"I don't know—"

"Cut the scene. Please." Her voice trails off. "I have a daughter."

Pearl. When she's older she won't care whose fault this is. All she'll see is me on the screen playing her sad mother.

Peter drops his head. "I know that."

I almost believe that he'll cave in.

"I need to go talk to Viva. I'm sorry. I'll see you on set, Joss," he says. "Norah, I'll have to tell TJ you're coming. We don't want any surprises on set." Peter steps out the door.

In Norah's teary eyes I see that even though she's an adult, she's still TJ's little sister on the inside. And tonight that little sister is me.

"Fifteen minutes!" Benji calls through my screen door. I make a last wish for a way out of this. But when I see the wardrobe girl coming, any hope of that disappears.

"Norah, if I could have any wish, I wouldn't—"

"I know." She covers my hand with hers. We have nothing left to fight for or with.

"Monique's here to help you get ready," Benji says, letting Monique in.

On my laptop, Tatum is still frozen, wearing overalls and a satin hat. She's like a dragon inside a butterfly cocoon. I close the screen. Now I'll have to be scrappy without her.

Nobody talks after my fifteen-minute warning. It's so tight in this bathroom we don't bother to shut the door. Monique turns the shower on. I watch her turn the hot water up before adding the cold. I've never used a trailer shower before. This one is dingy and small and smells like that too-blue toilet cleaner that's always standing in the corner. Monique checks my outfit and backs up to let me step into the shower, fully clothed. But before I do, I see Norah sitting at the table reading tonight's lines. I don't want her to see that. It's hurtful. But she's already reading with her hand over her mouth. I can't stop her. I can't stop any of this.

I step into the shower and catch my breath until the water warms up. Then I hold my head under. The water smells like plastic and rust. I tip my face down to keep it out of my mouth. The script runs through my head, and I know that at the same time, Norah is reliving the real night in her own mind. Tears build in my chest. I hold them back with all my might.

Stepping out, I wrap a towel around my body as Monique dries my feet and wriggles my sneakers on. The next person to enter my trailer is Louie, the sound tech who's here to attach my mic. Norah is still holding the script. Bending it. Folding it. Creasing it. I can't look at her face. If I do, I won't be able to hold back my tears anymore.

I grab on to the mic so Louie can drop the battery pack and the wire down the back of my wet shirt. My shorts are too flimsy to hold the pack, so he tightens an elastic belt underneath my clothes.

Benji knocks. He's ready whenever I am.

Louie still has to clip the mic somewhere on my shirt. I hope it takes him a long time to find the right spot. The longer the better. But he tucks the mic right under my collar, clips it there without a hassle, and he's done.

As Louie steps away, I glimpse Norah and me in the mirror. Her chin that looks like mine is held high. At this moment I know deep in my gut that I want to grow up to be just like her. I've never felt this way about my mother.

Monique hands me a sweat suit to put on just to keep warm. I take it without so much as a nod. She's just another half a grown-up who seems to care but is useless when it really counts. The hoodie says MONTAUK on the chest. The bottoms say THE END across the butt. I pull the sweats over my wet wardrobe. It's time.

. . . . .

Our basecamp is lit by spotlights like it's part of the movie, too. The craft service table is set up right next to my trailer. I can smell freshly baked cookies. If this was an order from Terrance, it doesn't mean anything to me.

Following Benji down to the beach trail, I hear Terrance's voice crackle through Benji's walkie-talkie. "Is the Bessie ready?"

162

Benji presses the button and answers, "We're walking."

Up ahead are Chris and Terrance, ready and waiting. I keep my eyes down to avoid Terrance, but when he comes up and pulls me aside, there's nothing I can do.

"You're my firecracker, kiddo. You know that, don't you?" he says.

Nothing at all . . . nothing at all . . .

"We've got the camera on the crane and we've set up another on the beach so we'll shoot two angles at once, all right?"

He's trying to make this quicker, easier—the more angles we cover at once, the fewer takes we'll need. But what does it matter now? After the first bullet, I doubt you can even feel the second or the third.

"I know this is a tough one, but you can do this," Terrance says. "You're the only Norah I ever wanted."

I hate these wet clothes that are now seeping through my dry clothes. I'm shaking. I can't control it if I try.

Terrance presses something into my palm. "Here, take this. It's for good luck. If you're in a tough spot, just hold on to it and use everything you're feeling and push through."

It's a piece of brown sea glass from the butt end of a bottle. Terrance isn't just a liar. He's also an unoriginal gift giver. I look up for a last word from Chris, but he's already headed up the trail with Benji. The next time I see him he'll be TJ and I'll be Norah.

163

. . . . .

I start running even before Terrance calls action. Thin strips of glow-in-the-dark tape guide the path down to the beach. I can hear my heartbeat and my breath. The camera on the accordion crane rustles through the branches overhead. For a second I actually think I can outrun it. I speed up, farther and faster. *I can do it. I can outrun Terrance and Peter and my mother and the camera. I can outrun my life.*

"Norah!" I hear. There's no escaping. I'm in this scene now, doing it exactly the way everybody wants me to do it. "Norah! Stop! Stop! What's the matter?"

The path opens. I burst out of the trail toward the endless black ocean and run until I stumble in the sand and fall to my knees. The second camera is waiting on the beach. There's no getting away no matter how fast I run.

"Norah!" Chris drops beside me. "God, you're soaking, you're shivering." In a second, I feel his flannel shirt around me; the warmth, the softness, the comfort are real, but I can't wrap it tightly enough to vanish inside of it. "What happened?"

Covering my face, I sputter, "I can't . . . I can't say it!"

"It was him, wasn't it? He did something to you?"

"Don't make me go back there, TJ, please." I squeeze handfuls of sand to grab hold of something, anything, but the sand keeps slipping, slipping, slipping through my fingers. "I can't go back there."

"We won't. We won't. I promise." He brings his face close to mine. "But you have to tell me, Norah. You have to. What did he do?"

My eye catches movement behind the monitor—somebody tall and round, rocking from side to side.

"It's okay," Chris says.

Rodney's here, he's here, I want to tell Chris. *I didn't even think of him coming.*

"Whatever it is, just say it," Chris says. Our eyes lock.

How can I do this with Rodney watching me?

I cover my ears as if I can stop from hearing my own voice. "He was in the shower. And he was yelling at me to bring him a towel . . ." I've got so much hate inside me that I'm trembling. "He kept yelling and screaming that I'm supposed to replace the goddamn towels when I do the laundry . . ." I bury my head and clutch my shins.

"Then what? What, Norah?" Chris puts his hand on my back. "What did he do?"

I shake my head against these words and every single person who's forcing me to say them. Feeling the dim spotlight against my face, I swallow hard and try to let everything out. "I was in the doorway with the towel . . ." *Spill it. Spill it. Get it over with.* "I could see him behind the curtain . . . He kept yelling, 'Well, bring it to me. Get the hell in here.' I didn't want to go in there . . ." *One take. One take. Say it! Say it!* "But he was screaming so loud, I went in." *It's just me and Chris. Just Chris and me.*

"He grabbed me, grabbed me and pulled me in. I was slipping, I didn't want to open my eyes, I didn't want to see him. But he pulled me up in front of him . . . and the water was so hot . . ."

Chris is shaking now, too. He's punching his knee and breathing hard while I try to go on with Rodney staring. The moment I say it, Rodney's going to picture me in front of him, and I'm going to be known as this girl forever.

I brace myself to push the lines out. And then, through the words and the breaths between them, I feel like Norah.

"He said, 'Shut up. Quit crying. You're not a baby anymore. So you might as well make yourself useful from now on.' I didn't want to be in there, TJ. I didn't want to see him. I was trying to get away, but he held me there . . . He *made* me touch him. He *made* me do it."

Chris pulls me into his arms, bringing me back into myself and out of Norah. I rub my hands in my lap to wipe myself clean from this dirty thing I've said, from this dirty thing that Norah was forced to do.

"Please don't make me go back," I blurt through my tears.

Chris chokes back his own tears. "I'm sorry. I'm so sorry, Norah," he sputters. "I should've been there. We won't go back. I promise." He holds me closer, and I know that it's really Chris hugging me, and he knows that it's the real me who's hugging him. "We're not goin' back."

I'm crying so hard for me and for Norah when she was

little and for Norah now that I can't stop. If I squeeze my eyes against the light, maybe the camera will be gone when I open them.

"She got it," Terrance says from behind the monitor. "That was it. That was Norah. Cut!"

"You did it, Joss. It's over." Chris tucks his chin to whisper in my ear, under the strength of our mics. His tears slide down my earlobe. "Screw all these assholes. To hell with them. Everything's for *us* now," he reminds me, smacking the sand. "It's all about *us* from here on."

"Checking it . . ." Terrance calls.

Everyone holds still while we wait for Terrance to check if the tape is any good. But the ocean is moving—it's rolling and crashing, rolling and crashing—even "Cut" can't make it stop.

"Did you get it?" I grit my teeth from the cold or anger. Both. "Did you get what you need, *TJ*?"

"Beautiful, Joss. It's perfect. We got it!"

My tears sting. I run to Norah in the warming tent where I asked her to wait. I didn't want her on the sidelines or watching the monitors. She didn't need to see all that. Norah hugs me without a word as Monique wraps a heated towel over my shoulders. The towel doesn't make a difference; I'm colder now on the inside than I am on the outside.

This was the first emotional scene I've ever done without using a trigger. But the next time I need to remember a terrible moment, I'll just think of this.

"Joss!" Terrance calls, catching up. He ignores Norah, who's stiff as a soldier beside me. Either Terrance is crying or his eyes are shining from the moonlight. Either way, I know that he will never, ever cut the scene. "Wow, kiddo. You were so, so—"

I push his heavy hand off my shoulder and run with Norah straight up the path toward the trailer. Terrance got what he needed. I'm done here.

16

Don't think for a second that I'll forget this.

My mother's note is written on the back of Chris's:

Joss is in my room. —Chris

It's mother/daughter double-crossing on one piece of paper.

Viva's makeup bag and toothbrush are gone, so it's official. I've got the room to myself for the night. But if I got what I wanted, then why do I feel so lousy?

"Joss! Joss!" Someone's pounding on my door. "Open up!" It's Jericho pushing his eye close to the peephole and Chris standing with him.

"What are you guys doing?" I open the door and squint at the overhead light with the mosquito corpses frying inside it.

"We just saw Viva hangin' on Terrance all the way to his room!" Jericho cackles.

"I know. I know. That's what you came to tell me?" I shake my head and start to close the door. "Haha. It's so funny. My mom's a big whoretauk. Big deal."

"No." Chris stops the door with his toe. "We came to tell you that you're free. Get dressed." He grins. "You're coming out with us."

. . . . .

The local kids flick their flashlights on once the streetlamps are far behind us. The path isn't much. The grass on either side is as high as my hip. Ray and another boy are up ahead. Me and Jericho and Chris are in the middle, and Arianne and Ray's girlfriend, Keri, are behind us. The sound of the ocean is fading under angry crickets. My ears itch from the sound.

"You should go up and walk next to him," I hear Keri say to Arianne. I stick my elbows out to take up the trail. *Single file,* I want to tell her. *He's with me.*

"Where are we going?" I tug Jericho's shirt and whisper. "The locals don't like me. I shouldn't be following them into nowhere. Let's just hang out the three of us. Besides, we've got a surf lesson tomorrow. I don't want to stay out too late."

"Don't worry about it," he whispers back. "And if anything goes down, I got my dad's watch. It has a glow-in-the-dark compass."

"Should we be worried about ticks?" I zip up my sweatshirt even though I'm warm.

"No. We should be worried about murderers. The Long Island serial killer. I read about it online and in the *Daily Montauk*. They found bodies up and down this stretch of beach. All girls, some were prostitutes." Jericho slows and looks back at me. "About your size and hair color."

"Shut it," I say.

Chris pushes him on. "Keep walking, Jericho."

"I'm not kidding. The news is everywhere. Haven't you been reading the papers?"

What does he do? Read the newspaper with his coffee every morning? Once again, Jericho is the know-it-all and I'm the know-nothing.

"There *is* a Long Island serial killer," says Arianne. "It's true. And he is still out there."

"You mean, out *here*," says Jericho as we weave forward. "Serial killers always have a type." His voice gets breathier as the path gets steeper. "Criminal psychologists say that serial killers are probably killing the same woman over and over in their minds, usually their mother."

Now he's making sense.

"They think this guy might be someone in the community, a fisherman, maybe, because the bodies were found wrapped in fishing net. Some of them are so badly decomposed that they're *unidentifiable*. The killer is probably someone close. Someone very, very close." He turns and grabs me so fast I lose my breath, and Arianne and Keri scream behind me. Jericho lets go of me to put his arm around Keri. "Easy, easy. I'm just kidding around. I'm sorry." He walks with her, keeping his arm slung over her. "Don't worry, I'll protect you."

Voices up ahead are joking and laughing, but as we get closer, the voices hush.

"Approaching! Approaching!" Flashlights swirl in our direction, swinging from side to side.

"Who goes there?" somebody asks. "Friend or foe?"

"Friend!" Ray says as he leads us up a steep hill.

Keeping guard at the top of the hill is—no surprise—Gwen holding a flashlight and a walking stick tall as her. She is a top-of-the-hill kind of girl. "Hey! You said *friend*!" she yells, working her flashlight over the boys and me.

"They're friends." Ray points a stalk of sea grass at us.

"No. They're infiltrators!" she yells.

If she starts throwing rocks, I'm throwing them back. After the scene I did tonight, I'm allowed to be wherever I damn well please.

"Nah, just actors," Ray says.

"Yeah, an actor with an arm around your girlfriend." Gwen shines her flashlight behind me. "Keri, you traitor!"

Ray points his flashlight from Jericho to his girlfriend. "Keri, what are you doing?"

"Nothing, Ray! I swear!" She runs up the hill after him. "He was just being stupid. Don't be mad. Not now, when things are going so good."

"For who?" Ray yells. "Tell me, Keri. Who are they goin' good for?"

Leave it to Jericho—who's laughing his guts out—to break up a three-month romance.

"Way to bring the drama, actors!" Gwen stares straight into my eyes. "Approach at your own risk." She turns away, and I notice the gigantic concrete box behind her, sort of like a garage that's partially buried in the hill. Most of it's covered in graffiti, not fancy like bubble letters on subway cars, just scratchy stuff. Nothing you'd print on a T-shirt.

"What is this place?" Chris asks Arianne.

Arianne swoops in on him, touching his arm with her fingertips. Now I know what *infiltrator* means.

"It's a World War II bunker," she says. "It's been here, like, forever."

How about, since World War II?

"Naw, for real?" Chris asks, fascinated.

"Come, I'll show you," Arianne says.

If you want my opinion, she's shown him enough already. But Chris is walking away with her, and Jericho is already talking to another local girl who's wearing a skirt that's so short it could be a tube top or even a headband. So now I'm all alone in the dark. I'm left standing here to get Lyme disease or serial killed by a fisherman when Arianne ends up with Chris—again!

I'm the one Chris came to get tonight. I'm the one he hugged through the very worst scene. How could I film something so disgusting, and then afterward, end up with nothing? I feel like starting World War III.

I keep remembering Jericho's stupid T-shirt from the other day. Is that all boys are? Hot dogs chasing buns?

"What, do you think you're cool or somethin'?" Gwen stares at me and holds a beer can at her hip. Her friends are crowding around.

"Do I think *I'm* cool?" I say. I want to bite this girl's head off. I can handle the Queen of Montauk now that I've stood up to Viva. "You're the one standing on a hill asking 'friend or foe' and waving your big stick!"

Gwen steps back and laughs, mocking me. Something snaps inside me, and if I don't let everything out, I'll blow. I gave orders to an executive producer today. I'm not gonna stand here and let the surfer girl make fun of me.

"I don't think I'm cool at all. I think I'm a Bessie." I widen my stance. "That's what the director calls me. Do you know what that is?"

Surprised, Gwen shakes her head. "Uh . . . no. What?"

"It's a *cow*. It's a piece of meat that Hollywood chops into little pieces so that they can make money off of it movie after movie." I clench my fists. "And then as soon as I'm not cute anymore, they'll trade me for magic beans. And it's *over* for me!" I yell and wipe my sweaty face with my arm.

Unidentifiable. That's what I'll be. Unidentifiable . . .

Gwen's eyes sparkle in the darkness. Her friends gather in a horseshoe around me.

"So what?" One of the Montauk boys shakes a can of spray paint. "You make a shitload of money."

"No, I don't. My mother does. For her dud business ideas." I rip a tall blade of grass out of the ground and tear at it. "The rest she puts away for my future, for when I'm a has-been."

"Your future? Ha! Right!"

"You better check under her mattress."

"You'll get your Coogan money," Jericho chimes in over the new girl's shoulder. "The Coogan Law is a rule that makes show-biz parents save fifteen percent for their kids," he explains to the girl. She gazes at him as if he's the smartest guy on the planet.

I cross my arms. "What's fifteen percent? I work a *hundred* percent!" I'm no math whiz, either, but I know what I deserve.

"True," Jericho says.

"I need this money, Jericho." I point at my chest. "I'm not like you. This isn't just *fun* for me!"

The locals close in on us. "Oh, boo hoo. Come on, you've got it made."

"Yeah, poor baby!"

"No, hey. It's true," says a boy with a flashlight hanging from his neck. "She needs to watch her back. Remember that guy from Nickelodeon? The one with the Mohawk?"

"Cameron Coombs!"

"Yeah! He's, like, homeless now."

175

"That's right! He's washing cars under the highway."

"I loved *Cameron's Truth about the World*," Jericho's girl says. "He's homeless? How sad!"

"Who cares?" The boy with the spray can steps forward. "You get to sign autographs and stuff."

"*Autographs?* You want my *autograph?*" I lunge at him and snatch the paint from his hand. Then I stomp up toward the bunker.

Reaching high against the concrete wall, I rise to my toes. I imagine I'm climbing a beanstalk up, up, up, all the way to Terrance's castle in the sky. The paint fumes hit me hard when I press the nozzle. I breathe deeply. I'm dizzy in seconds, spraying my loopy handwriting across the brass knocker on Terrance's fancy front door while he and my mother eat lobster at his long dining room table. They're laughing it up about what a klutz I was climbing through the deli window. He's wearing a tuxedo and bow tie. Underneath her dress, Viva's wearing a dance leotard that makes her magically appear ten pounds slimmer. They're toasting, "To Rodney and what a completely swell guy he is!"

But they can say whatever they want about Rodney. It doesn't matter to me anymore if it's true or untrue. If it's true? Good for him. If it's not? Good for me for telling him off. I'm done being pleasing.

The only thing that matters from now on is: No one. Is messing. With Joss Byrd!

MOO!
—CASH COW

I stumble back, thrilled and terrified by what I've done. I'm shocked at how bright, how red, how loud the letters are. The other kids shake their heads as they watch the W bleed down the wall. If I were sure how to spell Bessie, I would have.

"That's mucked up."

"A Hollywood tragedy."

"Make room under the highway."

Gwen steps forward, offering me her beer can. "Here. It looks like you need this more than I do."

I take it—my first beer—without thanking her, and in my second wow performance today, I pretend to drink it without gagging from the smell and this strange girl's saliva.

"But you're wrong, you know." Gwen's expressionless face comes very close to mine.

I want to ask how she got to rule the ocean and become Captain of Bunker Hill because I am going to be Captain of *The Locals*, Captain of the Byrd Girls, Captain of Hollywood!

"It won't be over when you're not cute anymore," she says. "They'll want something else from you then."

I think I know what she's about to say, and I don't want to hear it. But because she's talking to me now like we're actually friends, I ask, "What's that?"

Gwen pauses, unblinking. "*Sex*, stupid!"

And there it is: my destiny in two words. It's so obvious that

177

even a surfer girl from Montauk—the farthest possible point from Hollywood—knows it.

Gwen laughs. "If you don't pork out you could be objectified till you're at least thirty. I bet I'd hear about you then."

I look down at my hands that still smell of spray paint. I should've written "Doomed Kid Actor."

Suddenly Chris comes yelling from around the corner, "Would you quit it already with the pictures?" It's surprising to hear him raise his voice. "I mean it! I'm not some freakin' zoo animal."

"I'm sorry. I won't post them, I promise," Arianne says in a baby voice. "You're just so cute. I want to remember you. Won't you remember me? The other night was special, didn't you think?"

Chris is trying to walk away, but he can't shake her loose. I want to punch her in the gut.

"Chris!" Arianne huffs. "You can't just do what you did with me and then act like it never happened."

"Whatever. Just . . . sorry. Just leave me alone." Chris pushes through the other kids and makes his way over to the wall.

"Leave you alone?" She grabs his arm. "That's not what you said in the shed when I pulled your shorts down."

"Ohhh!" the other kids say.

Chris dares her with his eyes.

"You said, 'You're gorgeous, Arianne, you feel real good, Arianne . . .'"

"Shut up!" I yell, for me and for Chris.

"'. . . That's sooo good, just relax, keep going, Arianne.'" She lifts her phone and swipes the screen to show everyone her pictures.

Jericho rushes her. "Delete them, you bitch!" he yells. "Let me see you do it!"

"Get away from me!" Arianne twists away from him. "Get your hands off of my phone!"

"Leave it, man! It won't do any good," Chris yells. He picks the spray can off the ground, holds it next to my autograph, and sprays:

GRADE-A CHUCK BEEF WAS HERE!

"Arianne," Gwen snickers. "I thought you said he was vegetarian."

"Go to hell, Gwen!" Arianne cries, running off.

"Jericho? Joss?" When Chris calls us, we zoom to his side. "Let's go home."

Jericho charges ahead to lead the way as he ties sea grass around his forehead like a bandanna. The three of us dodge through the Montauk kids and make our way around the bunker. But at the top of the hill, we groan and scratch. Even with a glow-in-the-dark compass watch, we can't go anywhere without the locals because on our own, we can't see a thing.

17

"IN ABOUT TWENTY YARDS, I WANT YOU TO TURN AROUND and face the shore!" Terrance yells through a megaphone. Me and the boys paddle our surfboards toward a man in a safety boat that's waiting in the water. Beneath us there's three safety divers in gray wetsuits ready if any of us wipe out. I pretend that they're dolphins that I've raised from pups as their bubbles float up to the surface. If I fall they'll catch me and lift me up on their noses and carry me to shore.

I push farther into the ocean, head on, into the waves on my very best day—the one that will make up for the worst.

Fingers together . . . right arm plunge, push, and glide . . . left arm plunge, push, and glide . . .

"Lift up to let the wave pass underneath you!" calls Kato, our surf instructor who's floating on his surfboard beside us. "Just like yesterday's lesson. Pay attention. Head up, eyes on the horizon!"

I do a push up to lift my chest. My board reaches up and

over the lip of the wave. The water slips underneath me. The spray tickles my face. My neck feels tight and my arms are weak and noodly. The middle of the ocean isn't the best place to realize you haven't got any energy. I used mine up during yesterday's lesson, but I can make it through today on excitement alone. I caught a wave yesterday when Kato pushed my board into it. Today I'll do it by myself for the camera. Chris was right about this being the sweetest scene ever. And it's all for us.

Push up . . . up and over . . . plunge, push, and glide . . . Push up . . . up and over . . . plunge, push, and glide . . . must . . . start . . . exercising . . .

When I look over my shoulder, I see Terrance holding his hand up—far enough.

We all spin around to face the camera. It's standing on legs at the edge of the shore. Now I can take a rest.

"I want you to pick a permanent point in front of you on the beach and another marker at a right angle on the rock barrier." Kato stretches his lean, muscly arm to trace from the shore to the rocks.

I sit up and straddle my board. The boys do the same. Shielding the sun from my eyes, I choose a white sign on the beach, and on the rocks, I choose the pointy part that's white on the side.

"If you connect yourself to those points in your mind, it'll form a triangle," Kato says.

The sign and the pointy rock connect with me to make a triangle.

"That's your safety zone. Don't go any wider or farther than these two markers. Now we wait for the waves!"

I watched Kato surf while the crew was setting up this morning. He can bounce like his board is on springs and maneuver in and out of a wave. I even saw him spin a 360. I remember everything he tells us. The current is pushing me slightly to the left, so I lean to the side and paddle to the right to stay in my safety zone.

"Holy, yikes!" Jericho says. "We aren't the only ones who need a safety zone."

I look toward the shore, and I see what he means—a pretty, light-haired woman in a flowy white skirt is walking across the beach toward Terrance. There's no mistaking her. I've seen her in magazines and on the Internet. I even remember her from a frame in Terrance's LA office.

Mrs. Rivenbach.

"Oh, no," Chris says.

I hold my breath.

"I want you to check your safety zone constantly," says Kato. "Know where you are at all times!"

Three other points make a triangle: Terrance. Mrs. Rivenbach. Viva.

My mother is underneath the black tent, watching us on monitors. She's keeping away from the others on the sand because she's still sore about being booted off the set two nights ago.

Don't you dare freak out, Viva. Please don't embarrass me during my last scene.

"If you float away from that triangle, you're out too far, and it can mean big trouble," Kato says as Mrs. Rivenbach walks past the white sign.

Big trouble.

Mrs. Rivenbach runs up to Terrance. He sees her. She sees him.

Viva turns her head. She sees them both.

Terrance hugs his wife. He's talking to her now, probably telling her how happy he is that she's here, how nice she looks, how lonely he's been this whole shoot.

Liar! Liar! Liar! What does Terrance plan to do now, bring her with us to the lighthouse?

I'm gripping my surfboard so hard that I can't feel my fingers anymore.

"Be cool, Viva," Chris says.

If Viva has a fit we'll be done in this business just like Cameron and Oscar Coombs. Anyone on this beach—the locals, the tourists, even the crew—could take pictures or video. No director or producer from here to LA would work with us again.

My mother stares and stares at the lady in white. I stare and stare at my mother. If I stare hard enough maybe she'll read my mind.

Keep your hands off the blender, Viva. Please . . . please . . . please . . .

"Read these waves," Kato instructs us. Seagulls squawk overhead. "Do you see that white water? That one's about five seconds too late. You see the next swell? Three, two, one, that's when you paddle, paddle, paddle as hard and as fast and as deep as you can."

I need to pay attention. This isn't school. It's important. But I'm distracted worrying about my mother, who's now pacing behind her chair.

This is exactly why I had you kicked off set. Why do you make everything so hard?

"This isn't good," I hear Jericho say.

"You'll feel the movement underneath you," Kato says. "Then you'll stand, nice and easy, keeping your eyes up on the shore."

"We're rolling! Let's see one at a time!" Terrance calls. My mother is pulling her hair at the sound of his voice. The man in the safety boat repeats the roll; his words bounce off the water toward us.

Hold it together, just a few more minutes.

We hear "Action!" from the shore and then from the boat.

"You're up first, Joss!" Kato startles me to attention.

There's a swell speeding up behind me, pushing me forward. I lower onto my stomach and count. Three, two, one! I paddle, paddle, paddle with every ounce of strength . . . and glide!

"Now!" Kato says. "Get up, get up! Stand nice and easy! Head up, eyes on the shore, arms out!"

I'm up and I'm balancing and sliding across the sea. I'm brave and unafraid and free.

"Go! Go! Go!" the boys are hollering.

We have to ride this wave as long as we can . . . just ride it and ride it and ride it . . . as long as we can.

Eyes up.

Knees bent.

I stretch one arm in front and one arm behind, and I'm a surfer girl!

Everyone is clapping and cheering me on: Terrance and Peter and Benji and the whole crew, Jericho's dad, Grandma Lorna and Damon and strangers are calling my name. "Go, Joss! Go!" I know that even Norah, from up in her crow's nest, can see me. But way behind the black tent, Viva is walking away from Terrance and his wife, and from me.

"Lean forward, Joss!" Kato yells, suddenly.

I hear him, but I can't think fast enough to know what he means or figure out how to do it.

"Forward! Lean *forward*!"

The board slips from underneath me. It torpedoes, nose to the sky, blocking the sun for a split second. I fall into the water, bottom first, just as the board crashes down onto my head. Underwater I'm thrown forward then pulled under and folded backward, feet over head. Somewhere deep down inside me, the chill is everything I wanted. There's no way to fight. I'm too tired, too rubbery, to even try. The ocean tosses and churns me over and under, over and under, swallowing me into fizz and bubbles. I hold my nose as white noise whirrs in my eardrums—*I want my mom . . . I want my mom . . . I want my mom . . .* Hand over hand I climb up my ankle leash and launch myself toward the surface. Nobody else will save me—not even the dolphins.

18

WHAT I'LL REMEMBER ABOUT WRAPPING *THE LOCALS* IS this stiff neck and the throbbing. I think I've got a conc head; the knot is getting really big. My teeth are chattering so hard I'm afraid they might chip. As I pull a bright orange towel—the color of emergencies—around my body, Terrance's wife is rubbing my back, which feels babyish, but I let her do it because I'm getting cold and I'm headachy, and I could've died. And anyway, if my mother wanted to rub my back, she'd be here herself to do it.

Mrs. Rivenbach takes an ice pack from the medic and holds it against my head. Her gold bracelet of diamonds all around dangles over my forehead.

"That was quite a spill. You had us all scared to death," she says.

I did take quite a spill. And if I'd drowned, Viva wouldn't have even known about it. "Is this real?" I touch the bracelet. My mother would drool buckets over it.

Mrs. Rivenbach turns the links so that the clasp slides to the bottom. "It's called a tennis bracelet," she says, which doesn't answer my question. It also doesn't seem very practical, tennis-wise. Even Viva would agree.

Terrance whistles for attention. Then he waves his hands over his head. "First I want to say thank you to my crew. You've been my dream team, without question, the best I've ever worked with."

The group claps. I tap my fists together inside my towel.

"And thank you to the vilest bastard in Montauk." Terrance motions to a man who's stepping out from behind the production assistants.

I wouldn't have recognized Rodney if you paid me in tennis bracelets; he's shaved clean and wearing a checkered golf shirt and bright white sneakers.

"No, no. Not anymore!" Rodney waves the comment aside. "And I apologize for having to be that vile of a bastard, especially to these guys." He points to the boys and me. "If I'm blessed enough to work with any of you again, hopefully I'll be a superhero or a brain surgeon or something. I'm sorry, kids. You can call me Tom now, please."

The crew laughs and applauds.

He shakes hands with the boys, who are sitting up front. "Chris, damn, you were crazy good, man. Crazy good. You're a tremendous talent."

Chris stands. "Thank you. Wow, yeah, you too. I mean, wow. I was scared out of my mind."

"Ugh, I'm *sorry*." Tom holds his hands up as if he's getting arrested. "I'm normal. I swear. That fight scene killed me. I've got a bum shoulder and a trick hip. I don't tackle anymore. I do *yoga*," he laughs. "And I owe you some rice pudding! I felt like crap about that. I thought about it all night. Man, the look on your face . . . no hard feelings?"

"No hard feelings." Chris gives him a hug. Then he turns and gives me a doofy smile. "Check him out, Joss. It's *Tom*," he says.

Good for Tom.

Tom lunges toward me with a smile. But I step back, so he changes his handshake into a nod.

Good for me.

"And, finally . . ." Terrance pauses and clears his throat. "Thank you from the bottom of my heart, to the three greatest, most talented kids in the world." He stands in front of his cast and crew and raises a glass of champagne. The grown-ups are passing glasses around and pouring the rest of the bottle. But even though Jericho and Chris and me are the "most talented kids in the world," no one passes anything to us. "You've made this a heart-stopping journey straight to the bitter end . . . Joss!" He points at me, and everybody hoots and claps. (Everybody, except somebody who isn't here.) "Thanks for putting up with all my bull and . . ." he goes on, tearing up, "and for making all of this come true for me." Terrance coughs and rubs his eyes. "When I was a kid, the real Rodney told me I'd never amount to anything. But . . . but thanks to you . . . well . . . here we are." He shakes his head. "So, let's all raise our glasses . . ."

Chris turns to me without a glass to raise.

I shrug.

". . . to *The Locals*!"

"To *The Locals*!" All the adults toast. (All of them, except somebody who isn't here.)

"I'll see you all tomorrow night at the wrap party. Be there. No more weepy speeches, I promise. Just free booze!"

And that's a wrap.

"Pictures, kids!" Jericho's father pulls the cap off his camera and scrambles in front of us. "For Posterity!" he says. I don't know who that is, but she's got a heap of pictures coming her way.

We strike silly poses—me with an ice pack on my head, and the boys, still shirtless, flexing their muscles. Groaning, Tom lowers onto the sand in front of us and freezes in different robot positions. Who would've thought I'd have wrap pictures with him instead of with my own mother? We all swap places. Then we swap places again. How many combinations can there be? In school I learned a way to figure it out using multiplication or by making a chart with each person's initials, but I can't remember how, exactly.

Next, anyone with a phone or a camera steps in and out until everybody gets a chance to be in a picture. (Everybody, except somebody who isn't here and who, now, won't be in any of the wrap pictures.)

We keep trading spots until Tom drops out to refill his champagne glass and I'm left posing with just Chris and Terrance and his wife. Mrs. Rivenbach holds my ice pack and fixes my tangled hair behind my ears. Terrance stretches his arm over Chris until his hand settles on my head. Behind Chris's back, Terrance whispers to me through clenched teeth, "Joss, after this you should go check on your mother."

Anyone on this beach would think that the four of us are a family—the Rivenbachs from Los Angeles, California, who play tennis wearing diamond jewelry. And Terrance looks like the kind of guy who would've taken me to the lighthouse if he promised to. But that's Hollywood for you. It can make people believe the fakest things.

· · · · ·

In room 204, Viva is inside the bathroom, crying and kicking the cabinets. But if she thinks that her boo-hooing will make me forget that she ruined my best day, she's even crazier than she seems.

"Viva?" I call as I pick sand out of my ear.

No answer. Just more crying and slamming.

"We're wrapped. We're all done," I say coolly. "I caught a wave. You missed it, you know."

She's sobbing in a gulping way that even she couldn't put on for attention.

"I wiped out real bad," I say to make her feel guilty. "I hit my head. They put me in an emergency towel." But the sound of her smacking things around and then crumpling herself onto the floor makes my voice and my anger start to fade. "You should've seen it . . ."

. . . . .

"I don't want to get out anymore," I say, staring through the window. Right outside our limo, on the red carpet, there's too much of everything—too many cameras and flashes and bright dresses and ID tags swinging and all the people, so many of them shouting. "It's too busy. And everybody's going to stare at me."

"Give us a moment, please," Viva tells our driver. Then she turns to me. "Of course they're going to stare at you. Because you look so grown-up and glamorous and they all loved your movie."

I don't feel grown-up or glamorous. I feel jittery in my belly and light in my head. "I want to go back to the hotel and just watch it on the TV." I miss the hotel's cool, white sheets, and thick, quiet walls, and I want the chocolate wafers that Doris sent in a fruit basket.

"But the rest of the cast is waiting for you." Viva smooths the edge of my gown. "They want to see you dressed up. All you have to do is smile. And if someone asks who you're wearing, you say Betsey Johnson, and then you'll go inside to sit and watch. It'll be fun, you'll see."

I wrap my fingers around my seat belt. Lights are flashing quicker. Shouts are growing louder. Dresses are turning brighter. I'd like to see my costars and to watch the awards show inside. But how?

"What about this," my mother says softly. "Do you want to go out there as a character?"

"What do you mean?" I concentrate on the clasps on my silver shoes that are heart-shaped rhinestones.

"Let's make up a girl who wants every person in the world to see her. And you can pretend to be her. Wanna do that?"

I look at her hopefully. "Who should I be?"

"Um . . . Bebe VanWaterHausen!" She laughs and lifts a hand to me, presenting Bebe.

I hold back a giggle.

Viva pulls my seat belt away so that she can hold my hands.

"What is Bebe like?" I ask.

"Bebe has a twin sister, but they were separated at birth. And she thinks that if she walks the red carpet, her sister might recognize her and realize they're long-lost twins." My mother squeezes my fingers and looks me straight in the eyes. "You have to go out there, Bebe. It's your mission. All right?"

Outside, cameras are rolling by on wheels. If the cameras spot me, my twin might be able to see me. "All right."

"Ready, Bebe?" Viva rubs my arm. "You look absolutely faboo."

I hug my mother tight. We press together, poofy dress against poofy dress. She smells like salon. "Ready."

. . . . .

"I'm okay now, though." I tap the bathroom door. "The medic gave me ice."

If it were me crying, Viva would say "Don't you dare cry." But those don't feel like the right words now.

"So, it's party time tomorrow night. I bet there'll be some surprises. Jericho and his dad already rented a snow cone cart for everybody today. Can you believe it? Some wrap gift, huh?"

Leave it to Jericho to show up me and Chris in front of everybody. It must be nice to be able to spend your movie money on gourmet ice.

"The snow cone guy's even wearing a white uniform and a striped paper hat. I didn't get any yet. There's all different flavors. They have coconut. If you want to go, they're probably still there."

When I knock, she doesn't answer, not even to yell at me to get lost. I don't know what else to do but take out my phone. And I can't think of anyone to call except for Terrance.

WAT SUD I DO? I text. Big deal if he sees my spelling now. I don't care what he thinks anymore.

IS SHE OK?

CRING HARD

SHE'LL BE FINE.

CAN U COM?

I CAN'T. JUST STAY WITH HER.

The shoot is already over, but Terrance is still making me to do his dirty work. His answer—I CAN'T—stabs me in the chest because it isn't true. Terrance Rivenbach can do anything he wants. He just doesn't want to come. He doesn't care about me or my mother. *The Locals* is wrapped for him, and so are we.

"Forget him. He's just a blowtard," I say to the bathroom door, too softly for my mother to hear. ". . . We're on the same side again, aren't we, Viva?"

I hear her pulling tissues from the box and blowing her nose.

"We can go for lobster . . . if you want," I say. "It's our last chance."

After a few minutes it's so quiet on the other side that it's scary; Viva is anything but quiet.

"Viva?" I knock louder. *"Mom?"*

"I'm fine," she finally answers, sniffling. "It's just so stressful at the end of a shoot."

I let out my breath and lean against the door frame.

"You know me," my mother says. "I'm always worried about what we're gonna do next. I just hate to sit still. The thought of us running out of jobs . . ." She pulls more tissues and then unrolls toilet paper. "But don't you start getting stressed out, too."

"I won't," I lie. I don't know what's worse: filming *The Locals* or not filming *The Locals*. "We could work on dancewear-slash-shapewear. I could help you think of a name. Doris says marketing is all about branding." I try to sound hopeful.

"Oh, forget it. What's the use?" Viva blurts. "It's a stupid idea. All my ideas are stupid."

I hope not *all*. I've finished four movies now, haven't I?

"God! I'm such a screwup!" she yells. "When am I going to pull it together? Look at me . . . what a wreck."

I touch the door with my fingertips.

"I knew it wasn't forever." Her voice softens. "But I just . . . can't I have something good for a little while? *For me?* Is that too much to ask?"

I fill a glass of ice water for my mother and leave it on the bedside table. I also open the laptop on her bed. The screen flashes pictures Viva must've taken of the ritziest, most beautiful houses in Montauk: Lego-like homes with clean, sharp edges, country cottages with worn wood shingles and perfectly clipped hedges all around. These are the kinds of houses with names like Covington Manor or the Beaumont Green. My mother has always wanted a house with a name.

The slideshow stops when I wake the DVD. I skip to Viva's favorite scene in *Paper Moon* and press play. The character Trixie Delight is saying how hard it is to keep a man. "I don't know why, but somehow I just don't manage to hold on real long . . . So, if you wait it out a little, it'll be over, you know?"

I understand now that while I've been busting myself to play the director's sister, my mother has been working just as hard, maybe even harder, to play the director's girlfriend for as long as she could. I never knew before tonight that Viva knows exactly what it is to be an actor. Come Monday, we're both without a set to go to.

Even though the sun hasn't set yet, the day is over for my

mother and me. So I pull my hungry, sunburned, sandy, and knotty-haired self into bed. As I change into my pajamas under my covers, I knock my mother's *Vogue* magazine—the one with a model with cherry-red lips and a very tight bun—off the bed. I hate *Vogue* magazine all of a sudden; it's filled with Mrs. Rivenbachs posing in vineyards, wearing designer gowns, and holding genuine LV bags (not the imitations my mother buys off the street in Manhattan).

Who cares if bags or gowns or diamonds are real when people are fakes?

When I hear Viva turn the doorknob, I pull the sheets over myself and press the sore spot on my head to feel the hurt. I'm so ashamed that I ever wished away Viva's high heels and makeup. Terrance might have twinkly eyes, but they only hide how sneaky he is inside. My mother, who chases palm trees and daydreams about mansions, is who she is. And whatever comes and goes for us, I always get by because I am who I am—a dirt driveway kid who keeps shaking off the dust.

Now that I think about it, our apartment complex in Tyrone has a name; it's on the brick sign at the main entryway—Shangri La. That means imaginary paradise. I heard it in a song, once.

19

I DON'T KNOW IF CHRIS AND JERICHO ARE LETTING ME lead or if I actually am the fastest paddler, but I'm way ahead of them as we're heading out to sea. An extra-long night's sleep did me a lot of good. I can't decide which I like more, the sound of paddling or the feel of it—the whooshing and gliding, plunging and lapping.

The water is cold and extra rough today; it's splashing mini waves at us from every direction. But we're going to ride it— just the boys and me—at one of the local spots far away from where we've been filming. No instructor. No safety divers. No camera. Just us.

"Good spot!" Chris yells, as I settle over a calm patch. "Turn there!"

I dip my left toe into the water and paddle on my right side to spin around. And that's when I see it! Way over on my right, at an angle that must be too sharp to see from the shore, finally, there it is—Montauk Lighthouse with its light flashing and a broad brown band around the middle just like on all the post-cards and the souvenir plates and the T-shirts and the night-lights in the shops in town! I open my mouth to say something to the boys, but then I stop myself. I've earned the lighthouse. I don't want to share my thoughts with anyone.

"Whoa, nice view!" Jericho raises his arms. "Hellooo, Montauk!"

"Decadent," says Chris.

In my head I count, *One, two, three, four, wink. One, two, three, four, wink . . .*

Every five seconds, the lighthouse winks at me.

I sit up on my board. Then I close my left eye and hold my hand open underneath the lighthouse to make it look as if it's sitting right here in my palm. Curling my fingers, I close the lighthouse inside my fist.

There. Mine now.

Who needs Terrance when I've got myself a view like this? And in any case, most things look better from far away than they do up close.

"Joss! Look alive!" Jericho yells.

"Behind you!" Chris says. "Take this wave! It's perfect!"

I drop to my belly and paddle, paddle, paddle as if it's the last thing I'll ever do. I feel the swell, pop up onto my feet, and plant my stance. The boys cheer behind me as I rush over the water and through the air. The lighthouse is standing tall and proud like a standing ovation.

. . . . .

Two things . . . two things . . . acting and surfing . . . I'm good at two things . . . I tell myself all the way back to the Beachcomber.

I see my reflection in car windows as I walk through the parking lot. I actually look cool—like a real surfer girl. I've got water in my ears and sand in my crotch to prove it. I could pass for a local any day.

Even though the knot on my head is sore, I'm determined to balance this board on my head all the way up the stairs and all the way through my door. It's my last chance to show Viva that I'm an actor *and* a surfer. *Two things!*

When I make it up to the second-floor landing, I see that the door to 204 is wide open. I can make a real entrance. "Viva!" I yell. "Can you take my picture before I drop this? Hurry, hurry, hurry! It's heavy. This is just a rental, but Chris is gonna buy me the Hawaiian one I like with the yellow flowers!" I say, losing my breath. "I caught *three* waves today! Whaddaya think?"

I wanted to step into the room and ta-da! But I can't because our bags are blocking the door. Everything's packed and looks ready to go.

"Epic news, Joss! Epic!" Viva says, hanging up her cell phone.

My head and my arms can't take anymore, so I slide the board down and set it outside our door. Viva can knock the wind outta me harder than the ocean can.

200

"I think Sharon Zwick wants you for her next movie," she says, as if I know who Sharon Zwick is.

Viva is smiling so big it's hard to believe she spent most of the night crying. "I sent her a little video from the other day."

"You showed her the video of my *butt*?"

"Don't worry. She loved it." Viva holds her phone to her chest. "She thought it was adorable. And now she wants to meet you."

I want to know what kind of part it is. After Viva drew the line for *The Locals* and then erased it, people will think I'll do anything to stay a movie star.

Sex, stupid! I hear Gwen's voice in my head. *I bet I'll hear about you then!*

"Sharon Zwick already signed on Georgina Timmons to play the older sister. She's fresh off that HBO series. She's getting to be so gorgeous, that girl."

I've seen Georgina Timmons kiss on-screen and step out of a bathtub with her hair dripping, and I think that's her in a music video getting spied on in a changing room wearing just underpants. I might be okay as long as Georgina does the kissing and dripping and underpants wearing. I might still have time left—maybe two more years—to play a little sister. By that time I'd like to figure out how to draw the line myself.

"And get this." Viva pauses with her hands on her hips. "Are you ready?"

"I'm ready." I stretch my aching arms behind my back.

She grins at me sideways. "Oh, I don't think you are."

"Just tell me," I say because this can go on all day.

"It . . . is . . ." One of Viva's favorite things is a drum roll.

"It is *what?*"

"A roller boogie, seventies movie!" Her other favorite thing is any occasion where there's a disco ball. Viva jumps over two bags of laundry and a suitcase to hug me. "You and Georgina Timmons are going to be roller disco divas. Is that the coolest or what?"

"It's the coolest," I say. But how can I tell? Sometimes there's no way to know until I'm soaking wet, crying about being pulled into the shower. Or maybe there's no way to tell until years later when people still remember you having diarrhea against a tree.

"You won't believe what I bought after I got the call. I turned around and there was this tiny vintage store. It was like a sign. Such finds. I swear I can feel that this is going to be really something." She pours the clothes out of two shopping bags onto the unmade bed. "Isn't this the grooviest?" There's a suede bikini with orange beads hanging from it. "Everything you see here? One-hundred-percent authentic. Probably worn to an actual roller disco. Isn't it the most?" She holds up a yarn top that looks like two triangular potholders stitched together. "Sharon Zwick wants you in her office at five," she says. "So if we leave right after lunch, we'll be able to make it to Manhattan by—"

"Five?" I ask, sitting on the edge of the bed. "Five o'clock? *Today?*"

"To-*day!*" she sings the word in two high notes and drapes

the new old clothes over her chest. "I tell you, baby, timing is everything. I mean, how lucky can we be? One opportunity ends, another begins . . ." She unfolds a pair of patched bell-bottom jeans. "Aren't these far-out?"

"But the wrap party . . ." I rake my fingers through my matted hair. "I'm supposed to give Chris a surfboard and he's supposed to give me one . . . and I still have school . . . Damon was going to help me write thank-you cards for everybody." Viva was supposed to buy wrap gifts, but she never did. She'd better explain that to Doris because I definitely don't want to do it.

My mother's too busy now typing something into her phone to listen. She has that look in her eyes—she's chasing something. It's the same look she had when Tallulah Leigh was calling to her through the newspaper. She's moved way past the wrap party, way past Montauk Lighthouse. She's full-speed behind to 1975.

"Can you picture it? You and Georgina Timmons?" She holds her phone with a picture of Georgina up against my face. "It's just perfect, isn't it? You look exactly like sisters! The same face shape. The same freckles. Why didn't we ever think of it before? It's just so *obvious* now! I'm sure they'll have you meet right away so you can bond. Won't that be fun?" Viva slings a fringe purse over her shoulder and across her body and asks, "I can pull this off, can't I?" She takes yellow sunglasses out of the bag and puts them on me. She misses my left ear, so I adjust them. "Pick something out. Imagine walking into the meeting in one of these getups? Sharon Zwick will just die." Viva keeps saying *Sharon Zwick* as if she's trying the name on for size, too.

"Come on, Joss. Disco with me." She points her index finger up and down from ceiling to hip.

I want the Sharon Zwick job. Of course I want it. But it's hard to snap into a new character. Just like it's hard to dance on demand.

"Get up, you! Shake a leg and boogie! We have to start watching *Soul Train* videos." Through these pink-tinted lenses, my mother's transported back in time with a leather headband around her forehead. "Hey." Viva stops boogying and lowers down to me. "Terrance offered to call Sharon Zwick for us, to put in a good word about you. But I told him to shove it."

"Really?" I'm shocked. I thought she would do whatever it took for me to work again.

"We can do it ourselves, can't we? This whole Hollywood thing?" Her eyes are asking me to believe in her. And this time, I think I do. I should. We're partners.

"Yeah," I say proudly.

"So, come on. Dance with me!" Viva waves beaded necklaces in the air. She invites me with a soft hand, and because she looks so refreshed, so optimistic, and so silly, and I don't want to bring her down, I stand and join her by "hitchhiking" with my thumbs.

"There you go." She smiles with her whole face, so I swivel to the left and then to the right. "That's my girl!"

We dance together in the mirror; I look like a totally different person in these sunglasses. This new girl in my reflection could be my 1970s self. Or she could have ironed hair parted perfectly down the middle or maybe feathery at the sides like I've seen in those grainy old camp movies Viva likes.

This imagining—Who will my character be?—makes me feel like a real actor.

Singing with her full voice now, Viva spins me under her arm. She points to me and sings that I'm the "Dancing Queen." She's the happiest I've seen her since I first got the part of Norah because there's nothing brighter than what might be ahead, especially if it's a disco ball.

· · · · ·

At lunch, saying goodbye to Terrance, the crew, and Jericho and his dad kind of felt like a long time coming. When you're ready to leave someone, they seem to fizzle away almost as soon as you unfold the hug.

Peter said there are wrap gifts, but they won't be ready until the party, so he'll have to mail mine. I'm glad for that because I haven't got anything to give people in return. I don't even have cards, since I didn't have time to make them with Damon.

Viva wrote an excuse note to get me out of the rest of my tutoring hours. Damon was nice about it, but he'd bought these really nice packs of blank greeting cards; they were thick with raised edges. They probably cost a lot. I offered to pay him back, but he wouldn't let me. He wished me luck with Sharon Zwick. Then he told me that I'll be just fine if I stick to Vern LaVeque's method and record my dialogue from now on. He also said I should get audio books and record my class lessons. I listened. And I thanked him—from my ears, to my heart, to my mouth.

I should've gotten everyone a box of delectables as a gift. That would've been easy enough. It's too late now. Except for Chris's surfboard, I only bought one Montauk souvenir this whole time, but it isn't for the cast or the crew.

And now it's down to Chris and me walking back to the Beachcomber very, very slowly, while he chews on a blade of sea grass. He's letting the end hang out of his mouth in kind of a cool way—like a cigarette but not a cigarette. The beads on my one-hundred-percent authentic seventies top click and clack as I walk. I can't read what's on Chris's mind, but that's okay. We don't need words to hold us together when we're the only kids on Earth who know what it's like to play a Rivenbach.

My truck isn't in the resort parking lot. But I do see Viva leaning up against a shiny, new red convertible with the top down. Our bags and my new surfboard are on the ground, waiting to be loaded.

"What is this?" I'm almost afraid to go near it.

Viva twirls a keychain around her finger. "It's a Mustang. Do you like it? Isn't she *everything*?"

I look to Chris and then back to my mother. "Is it . . . *ours*?"

She lifts her sunglasses onto her head. "Well, of course it's ours!"

"Where'd it come from?"

My future, I'm guessing.

"The dealer down the road."

"Do you need some help?" Chris picks up a suitcase and drops it into the car.

"That would be so lovely, Christopher. Thank you," Viva says, practicing manners that match the new car and being the kind of woman who doesn't lift her own luggage.

"But where's the truck?" I ask.

"Traded it." She leans on the hood and presents the car like on a game show.

It would've been nice to know she was trading the truck. What if I'd had something in the glove box or under the seat? She probably didn't even check. We rode for a lot of years in that truck. We sang duets in it and had McNuggets and Slurpees in it. I might've just wanted to see it go. One night we drove it to the edge of the park during the Summer Drive-In Series and watched the movie without paying. We couldn't hear the words but the ones we filled in cracked us up the whole time.

"Saucy, huh?" Viva asks.

"Well, it's definitely *you*," I say. Chris knows what I mean— it's loud, flashy, flips from cruisin' to hold-on-tight in two seconds. "Did you name her?"

"I just told you." She rubs her leg up and down the head-light. *"Saucy."*

I can't help but laugh. Maybe a convertible will be even better for the drive-in.

Chris tosses the last bag into the backseat but leaves my board out for me to load. We couldn't trade surfboards at the party the way we'd planned. But we went to the surf shop together before lunch—one last thing we got to do together.

"Now, say your goodbyes." Viva slides into the driver's seat. "You know how it's done."

"Quick like a bandit," I answer.

"That's right. Bye now, Christopher," she says, lowering her sunglasses back over her eyes.

"S'long, Viva." He holds up a palm.

I've said enough goodbyes to know that it isn't forever. There'll be interviews together to promote the movie and a premiere party, probably next spring—same us in fancy clothes. There might even be another hotel with our rooms on the same floor and maybe awards ceremonies to go to, if *The Locals* is a hit. But I've also said enough goodbyes to know that it'll never be like this again.

"What are you doin' next?" I ask.

"Not sure yet." He drops the blade of grass and stomps out its imaginary butt. "But I'm reading a couple projects that sound pretty cool. My agent said scripts will be rolling in after *The Locals* comes out, too. Isn't that always the way? I can play soccer another year, right?" When Chris smiles at me it's the first time I notice that a smile can be sad. "Have a groovy time in the seventies." He pokes at the beads dangling over my belly, rattling them. "I hear Zwick is pretty tough. Tough, but cool, so show her what you're made of."

"I will. And it'll be a good change for Viva, I think," I lean in and whisper, "for me to have a *woman* director."

I memorize the sound of Chris's laugh. Then, looking at the ground to keep my voice from shaking, I say, "I feel like you're really my brother."

"It was worth it, then, right?" He gives me a bigger, sadder smile. "'Cause you got a brother, and I got a sister. That might not mean much to Terrance, but it means something to me."

"I know. Yeah, it was worth it," I say, and I mean it.

"I'll see you on the red carpet." Chris tilts his head and looks at me at an angle.

"Yup." I shuffle my feet.

"Keep your eye on the horizon. And never go past your safety zone."

"You, too."

Viva starts the engine and turns on the radio.

"Wait. I almost forgot . . ." I hurry to the car and rifle through my luggage for that one souvenir I found in the town shop. "Can you give this to Norah for me before you leave?" I ask, running the small wooden box over to him. "Ray knows where to find her."

"Sure." He takes the gift from my hands. "What is it?"

"You can open it."

Lifting the lid, Chris says "Wow" at the brass telescope—the pirate kind that pulls out into a long tube. He stares at it for a good minute. "I'll make sure she gets it."

There's nothing more to say about something we both understand through and through.

"Later . . . Chuck." I punch him lightly on the shoulder.

Chris waits a beat before punching me back. "Later . . . Bessie."

So that I don't cry, I step back to lift my surfboard up and onto my head until I feel the balance. The board presses against my sore knot; the pain reminds me how tough I am. I turn away toward the car, bracing my board with one hand and waving with the other.

"Keep your sunny side up, up! Hide the side that gets blue!" I sing, and I don't look back.

· · · · ·

I know that Montauk Lighthouse is getting smaller and smaller behind us. But no matter how far away we go, I can count five seconds and remember that it's blinking just like it did when I didn't visit it during *The Locals*.

Viva finds an oldies station on the radio that's playing something funky with a trumpet and bubble sounds. She's tapping her hand on the steering wheel to the beat. I can bet she's picturing bell-bottoms and roller skates in her wind-blown head because as I listen to this music, I'm starting to picture them, too.

I reach into the bag at my feet and pull out the Montauk hoodie that Monique gave me the night of the worst scene. When I zip it on, I feel something in the pocket—the good luck sea glass from Terrance. Now I see that it isn't brown; it's deep green like moss or seaweed, and it isn't smooth along the edges yet. It needed more time.

The song blows louder over the radio with horns and crisp hand claps. I unclip my seat belt and pop up onto my knees.

Viva yells into the breeze, "The wind makes you feel so alive, doesn't it?"

It does. I'm reappearing breath by breath.

"So saucy!" She laughs and waves a hand to the sky.

My hair catches Montauk in each strand. The sticky salt air feels and smells the same as the day I got here except it's a second skin to me now, the way Chris became my brother in my heart. Straining against the speed, I stretch up tall. I pull my arm all the way back and throw Terrance's sea glass as far as I can toward the ocean because there is no such thing as luck. There's only work and no work, grown-ups and kids, truth and lies, pretending and being, action and cut, Norah and me, Viva and me. Me.

Me.

Acknowledgments

I'd like to thank the star makers, dream breakers, and soul takers who made this book possible:

The wonderful Molly Ker Hawn, for believing in me. My editor, Katherine Jacobs, who treated Joss, Chris, and the Montauk kids with love and care. The entire Roaring Brook team, especially Claire Dorsett, Jill Freshney, and Elizabeth Clark.

Wendy Nelson Tokunaga, who critiqued my earliest draft. Whitney Gardener and Kathleen Glasglow, for sharing the debut journey with me. Everyone at On Location Education, for the nonstop adventure. The cast and crew of *Boardwalk Empire,* for all those days at the beach. Rhoda Fine, Hollywood's favorite teacher, for her friendship and her stories. Oona Laurence, Stefania Owen, and the unstoppable mother/daughter duos I've been lucky enough to work with, especially Evy and Ryann Shane, who insisted I write a book in the first place.

My family and friends, especially Aloha LeBlanc, Gail Crawford, Tracy Borelli, William Fielding, Jasmine Glennon,

Lily and John Fielding, Marina and Ciceron Opida, Rachelle Peñaflor, Xander and Rebecca Peñaflor, Bill and Gladys Fielding, Ninette Limpo, Jeannie Stratos, Stella Watala, Lidia and Joe Szelwach, Keri Pinzone, Sandra Weitzman, Gladimyr Sully, and Tanya Rubins, for rooting for me and celebrating so hard.

My brother, Joseph Peñaflor, for wondering when I was going to do this. The answer is now. My loving parents, Joe and Sarah Peñaflor, for always cheering the loudest even when instructed to hold all applause until the end. I love you. My sweet little Vera, who sat beside me, and my husband, Rob Szelwach, for more than I can say.

Thank you all.

We're happy now.